WISH HARBOR

And Other Water Stories

T. S. Cook

ISBN: 0615635512
ISBN-13: 9780615635514

THIS BOOK IS DEDICATED TO

MONIQUE

…as is my whole life.

CONTENTS

FERRYMAN

It was going to be Ted's last summer. He started telling people early.

No, they howled. Teddy, not you! Summers on the island would be dim and unlivable without you, without your special twist on the rum pump. It didn't matter what the Hungarian was calling it this year, the island had always been "Teddy's." It would not be the same without Teddy behind the bar. They were boycotting, they were petitioning. "To whom?" he asked. "To you!" they cried.

"Too late," he said.

He marveled at it. Kill a hundred million brain cells and you're a god. Ted Kirkpatrik, with his hey-pardner smile, salt-and-pepper beard, barrel chest, Hawaiian shirt, hand on the rum pump, Teddy had been deified. The more he pumped, the more they believed, the more their hearts clung.

He had been there ten years. This was going to be his last summer. He meant it.

The name of the island had changed again. Not the actual name, of course. The permanent name was Spear

Island. It was on the charts, just off the main channel, back in a group of low, sandy, skunk-cabbage-smelling orphans. When Ted called Deev, he had to use the proper name: *"Request crowd control on Spear Island, Code 3."*

There was a family that had once farmed the island before quitting in the sixties. Asparagus was what grew best in the sandy soil and asparagus is not a plant that gives up easily. All over the island you could find clumps of the stuff still poking up, but these were not the tender little green logs you buy in a bunch at the Safeway. These were tough and black and fibrous, hard to cut and mostly tasteless. Every now and then a spear went rogue. It sucked up all the good from the surrounding soil and strangled off the competition. A rogue can get three, four feet tall and as big around as your arm. That's where the island got its name.

It was also the source of the rumors, of course: That girls partying on the island who can't find a man (not likely), or can't find the right man, or who think men are pigs (most likely) will save up pats of butter from the baked potato plate, sneak off into the interior after dark, find a becoming rogue, butter him up, and take a meat-less ride.

How many times had Ted been asked: Is it true? Do they really do that? Sometimes he says yes with a wink. Sometimes no with a wink. The truth? He does find them, big old asparaguses cracked off at about the right height, or still standing, a little buttery.

They're all pigs. That's the truth.

Right now the Hungarian was calling it Shipwreck Beach. Before that it was Hideaway Cove. It stays one thing for as long as the river allows. Once every couple of years it rains hard in the Sierras. A few hours later, down it all comes through the Sacramento and the San Joaquin, gushing and foaming over everything but the highest levees. They say if a man could strain out all the Sierra gold that passed where he stood, he'd be a millionaire in ten minutes. Islands like Spear can go completely under. The bar and the docks twisted together into a mass of splintered pine and wire rope, a weird rough-hewn octopus that grabbed up everything in its way: The kitchen and restaurant. The plywood bar. The half-assed "Beach Volleyball Arena" and all the Bud Light crap that came with it. The old storehouse filled with cups and plastic spoons and Styrofoam plates and a million packets of catsup. It's something to see.

Then the Hungarian brought in the 'dozers, pushed all the junk together in a big heap back behind the willows, weaseled some shady kind of construction loan and built it all up again.

Of course, the Hungarian wasted nothing, not even river flotsam. This spring he equipped the Cousins with gallons of red and black paint, a keg of nails and some used-up manila line. For about a week they climbed around up there, on the very top of the junk heap, hammering and sawing and laughing and singing, having the time of their lives. Henri and Ulysses are first cousins, fresh out of Haiti. Zero body fat and skin so black it cooked blue in the local sun. They cut and nailed and shifted that debris to look like the stern of a pirate ship, tossed by Caribbean surf onto an asparagus reef. When the black-painted hull with a red shear stripe was finished, Spear Island Resort became "Shipwreck Beach." To the Cousins it wasn't work. They were boys again, back home on the Isle of Pines, conjuring painted forts from driftwood, only this time being paid Yankee dollars for it, plus a ration at the pump.

These were the days Ted enjoyed, sort of. Before the summer and the endless mobs and noise and bullshit. Just Henri and Ulysses and himself, and a few hard hats finishing up the plumbing. Even these guys were okay in that pre-season, when the bar was just a place to cool off. Of course, they'd be back a few weeks later as paying guests, splintering the new dock with their slabs of over-powered fiberglass, transformed into hats-turned-backward horn-dogs by the witching presence of titty.

Henri and Ulysses had wives in Stockton. They went home at dusk. Juliet, the buck-toothed cook, came over for a few long days in the pre-season to scrape down the frying surfaces and swamp out the coolers, but she too was across the water by dark in her husband's fishing skiff. Only Ted stayed overnight on the island.

Three summers ago the Hungarian saw an old cruiser for sale down in the Bay. Thirty-foot ancient Chris Craft, wood, a mess, a stink in the bilge like a vomit of bad clams. This he had delivered to Spear Island and lashed to an old dock on the back side. "ZomeZing nitze for you, Tezzy," he said. "Manager's Residence" was painted on the side.

The cabin of the "Residence" was so leaky and damp that Ted kept all his stuff in plastic bags. This included his blanket and pillow and the "66-30" sweats he slept in. The "66-30" was a bar on the Arctic Circle, in Alaska, where he had worked for a couple of years, in season. Mostly locals, loggers and guides, fishermen in season and tourists. A girl named Lucy. A Greek owned that place. The pump was vodka.

Ted went up on deck in his "66-30's" and settled in for the last event of the day. He'd filled the flask earlier at the bar, the bottled stuff, the good stuff. The flask is a stainless steel job, nice, with his name engraved on the side, "Teddy." That's all. Just his name.

In two weeks, when the season starts, he won't have time for this. He'll be working until dawn every night, cleaning up after the thing, and be up at lunch time to help Juliet feed it. You start that kind of day with a hangover and you're dead. He'll be so tired most nights he'll crash in his clothes.

But these days, when there's this patch of time, he needed a pump of his own, one with his name on it. Ten big swallows. The cabin was just two steps down. The berth was big, he rarely missed it. This was his last summer.

The thing began with a roar. Literally. Six local guys off two half-scale cigarette boats. First ashore, first rum, first spewing drunk, first to remind Ted what he means to them. "The last fucking free place in this fucking country," they declared it. Hardly an original thought. It was something Ted had heard every night for ten years from staggering fools who thought the thirty yards of backwater channel that separated Spear from the rest of California were the Straits of Gibraltar.

The locals were just the preliminary. Come June, they started arriving in serious numbers, by the hundreds on daddies' boats, to line up four deep along the bar and clamor for their ration of fun. There was no off time, really, but between Thursday afternoon and Saturday at one AM (when the island had to clear by law) came the peak of the stampede. They thronged through the tin-roofed bar and restaurant, posed themselves under the dozens of *palapas*, gulped fluid tons of sugar and alcohol or Mexican beer swimming in fruit, choked down thousands of burgers that oozed orange grease, flopped hard to the volleyball sand in the throes of "Most Interesting Man in the World" hallucinations, jerked themselves around the concrete dance floor under the imaginary gaze of MTV cameras, sliced up their toes on buried glass, felt no pain, felt each other up, punched each other out, threw up on each other, and then cranked up their excessive Evinrudes on a projectile fling back across the dark river. Or, if daddy had bought the big model, stayed overnight at the dock and laid up in the cuddy cabin, contorted into fiberglass berths in ways only an anesthetized body could forgive. Sleeps four, fucks eight.

The temp crew that the Hungarian had hired this summer was no better or worse than last summer's. In fact, the bouncer was the same Yosef, a huge wrestler from UC Davis. Bright enough, big enough. Blonde Jane worked with him behind the bar. She wasn't a very fast hand and could *not* be taught how to spot a counterfeit twenty, but she never wore anything more than a bikini and that kept the worst of the droolers at her end.

Ted spun plastic cups under the rum pump with the broad smile and dexterity that had made him a Delta legend, but a cold misanthropy underlaid every motion. By the end of the third week, he was wrung out, dead tired, blank. How many more nights could he watch this circus? How many more times could he listen to their cloying patter? "Did you just cast a spell on me?" "Demon Rum ordered me to come over here and be your best friend." How many more times could he be trapped in a corner of the bar by a loser who had found solace in hazy theology. "We've all got God inside us, Ted. We're all a church all in ourselves, you know?"

How many more times could a man nod and agree? That the government is not telling us all it knows. That there's this conspiracy. That women are all bitches. That all men are dicks. "You know, Ted. You know that's right."

"I know."

Some night, some night soon, he'd start screaming and never stop. Thrash the bar clean of shot glasses and bottles. Start at one end and point each one out for what he was. Loser. Asshole. Cunt. Worthless. Teddy Kirkpatrik goes mad, the psychotic end of a Spear Island fixture. Popular bartender found floating in the backwater, beaten to shit by underage drunks.

It might be worth it.

Then, one Saturday night in late June, things subtly changed.

After dark, it was impossible to see who was landing at the far end of the dock from the brightly lit bar. So people listened. Usually what they heard was the eager rubber tramp of a handful of guys in sneakers. Handfuls of guys in sneakers made up eighty percent of the Spear clientele. That night they heard a rare thing indeed: the sound of women, a half dozen of them, arriving unattached.

Yosef's job was to stop the young-looking customers and ask for ID. The unspoken rule was that only guys got stopped. No one, not the Hungarian, not Yosef, not Ted wanted to discourage girls who had come all the way out to the island. The bald truth of it was that a more even ratio of men and women insured better behavior on the part of both. So when the new arrivals tripped happily up the float ramp, Yosef waved them through without hesitation. Yosef saw what everyone in the more-or-less hushed bar now saw. These were new girls. Nice girls. Pretty but not tarted up. The five of them settled in at a bar table and one of them came over to order. The crowd parted. She smiled at Ted warmly and said she'd heard about this famous rum punch on tap.

"First time on the island, darlin'?"

"Yes."

"Then this round's free. I'm Ted."

"I've heard of you, too."

"How many?"

"Five, please."

"Five it is. How'd you get over?"

"Pardon?"

"Get over the river?"

"The ferry."

"The ferry? What ferry?" Ted asked, as he slid five pumps her way, but she was already engaged in conversation with a young guy next to her. The guy carried the freebies away and that was the last Ted saw of her or her friends for the rest of the night. They might have had more to drink but they sure didn't have to pay for or carry any of it.

Finally the place cleared out, all boats gone home for Sunday morning as the law required. About an hour after last call, Ted saw Yosef on his way to his Alumicraft skiff and the ride home. "Easy night," Ted commented.

"Yeah," the wrestler replied. "Helps when there's more women."

"Night." Ted let him go.

Ted stayed up a while longer. About three he heard the growl of an outboard and saw the shape of a River Police Patrol Whaler 21 glide past the harbor entrance. A powerful halogen searchlight swept the dock. Ted lifted the hinged end of the bar and walked back to the main cash register. Above it hung a VHF unit set to channel 16.

"Spear Island station to River Police launch. That you, Deev?"

"It's me, Ted. All cleared out?" Rob Devareau was the senior field officer on the River Patrol. He was part cop, part traffic controller, part environmental watchdog. A good guy. Everyone called him Deev.

"Tie up, have a nightcap," Ted offered. It had happened in the past, rarely, but Ted always offered.

"Not tonight. Miles to go," came the reply. "Thanks anyway. Launch 1, clear." The Whaler foamed away. Thirty seconds later its running lights disappeared around the river's bend. Ten minutes later, Ted's lights were out.

Next Friday night the girls returned. They were not the very same group as before, although Ted recognized the sweet brunette who had ordered at the bar. There were new girls with her but they all were the same in that same...what?...fresh way. If the truth be told, many of the girls who regularly came to the island did not have that quality. They had to find a way over and Ted knew very few girls who owned their own speedboat. Hitching a ride with some guy, or group of guys, was an implied bargain. A lot of his regular girls were known as good-timers. Island girls. Asparagus girls. It's how the fights started: "She'd rather fuck a vegetable...."

No, these girls were different. The new arrivals were subsumed by the bar crowd as soon as they stepped off the ramp. An hour passed before Ted saw the brunette appear at the bar. He went right over to her.

"Hello again, darlin'," Ted said as he polished the bar. "Glad to see you came back."

"Hi," she replied. "I wanted to tell you, the ladies bathroom..."

"Yeah, I know, it's backed up. I've got Ulysses working on it."

She smiled. "I'll be so grateful if he fixes it, I'll read his book again."

"This Ulysses is from Haiti. Can I ask you something? Last week, I think you said you took the ferry over here?"

"Tonight, too."

"I never heard there was a ferry."

"Well, it's not like the Sausalito ferry. Just a guy with a boat."

"Where do you get this boat?"

"What's it called? Rincon-ers...?"

"Rinaker's Landing? In Stockton?"

"Right."

"What does he charge?"

"Nothing. Free."

Just then a blue-black shadow passed behind the crowd and gave Ted a thumbs-up.

"The toilets are running now, darlin'. I'll give you a thirty-second head start before I announce it."

"You're *my* classical hero," she whispered, winked, and bolted from the bar.

Ted watched her make a mannered but determined sprint to the restrooms and laughed. She had class. It wasn't that he was interested in her romantically. That was a ridiculous notion: forty-something Ted the Pump who lived in a half-sunk boat and one of these college girls. Even one of the local girls. Just how ridiculous the notion was had been demonstrated the first year he had worked on Spear, the lesson repeated every year thereafter. What intrigued him most was the ferry. It was unexpected, and anything unexpected was a balm.

Ted didn't see the brunette again until much later that night. About one AM he heard a blast on a fog horn. It was one of those compressed air deals that small boats are required to carry. He heard them all the time; blasting off air horns was a favorite pastime of the hats-turned-backwards crowd. This, however, was just a single sharp note, a signal. A few minutes later, Ted saw that evening's contingent of girls from Rinaker's Landing walking down the ramp toward the main dock. A wisp of imploring horny guys trailed behind them but the girls were clearly intending to take their ride home.

Ted called for Bikini Jane to cover and ducked under the hinged section of the bar. He walked swiftly along the embankment parallel to the main dock, matching his progress to the girls'. They stopped at the end of the furthest float and waited. Out of the darkness came a medium-sized I/O, a 22- or 24-foot Bayliner or Chapparal, open cockpit with lots of seating. The man at the wheel brought it gently to the dock, wrapped a single breast line around a cleat and held it there expertly while his passengers boarded. Only running lights were burning. The cockpit was in shadow. Ted could not see any detail of the ferryman except that he was tall, thin, and darkly dressed. With his angelic cargo aboard, he slipped the line and swung out into the channel, where the darkness of the river soon swallowed them up.

Another week passed. The girls from Rinaker's, as he was now calling them, kept coming. Different ones, the same ones. He would talk to them when they came up to the bar. How did they find out about this ferry?

"I don't know, my girlfriend knew about it."

"Just this summer the word started going around: if you want to get out here and party but you don't want to have to go with some guy and have him crawling all over you, the ferry is how."

So, no guys allowed?

"Yeah, that's, like, sort of the deal."

"I like the ride better that way."

What's name? Who is he?

"Don't know."

"Never heard his name."

And you never asked?

"I tried to talk to him once. He was nice but he said, 'Excuse me, Miss, but I need to pay attention to the river.'"

"Yeah, 'pay attention to the river,' that's what he says."

What does he look like?

"Tall."

"Thin."

"Nothing special."

Okay, nothing special. Some nice guy with a boat. Certainly nothing that should occupy a guy like Ted. Nothing that should, given his exhaustion, keep Ted from falling asleep immediately when his head hit the pillow. Or keep him half awake, half listening for another hull out there, other than his own, lapping the soothing water, coming his way.

Half listening, he heard the cry for help. It was a plea for rescue but it also carried a high overtone of pain. It woke him up just before dawn on a Saturday morning after a particularly busy Friday night. It was a woman's voice coming from the b-side of the island, some distance back in the pirate ship and rogue spears.

Ted pulled a waterproof shell over his sweats, took the six battery Maglite from its holder and started down the long dock. At the first part of the embankment he made a hard right into an overgrown path laden with moisture. There were ten yards of this stuff, soaking his pants and shoes, until he came clear of it and intersected the main path. The crying continued, but it was much closer now. Ted clicked the light on and began picking his way around piles of decaying debris, wood, tin, cardboard, Styrofoam. It was a maze and in the very center he found her. She was maybe twenty years old, Asian, curled up in the tightest fetal ball possible.

He touched her shoulder. He expected her to withdraw even more but instead she relaxed and looked up, her eyes expectant.

"Don't be worried, I'm a friend," Ted said softly. "What's wrong?"

"Where is this?" she said with some effort. Her teeth were chattering at a drummer's pace.

"Whoa," Ted cautioned, "you're hypothermic, darlin.'" He stripped off his windbreaker and held it out to her. "Put this on. Let's get you warmed up." The girl did as he suggested. "We'll go back and get some hot coffee in you, okay?"

"Where is this?" she asked again.

"You don't know where you are? This is Spear Island. I'm Ted, I'm the manager. Did you come here with someone?"

She looked at him, her face at one moment blank and the next moment contorted in confusion and fear. "No...I don't remember. I...I can't remember anything."

"What's your name?"

"Lisa. Lisa Chin."

"There you go, you remember that."

"But what happened? I..."

At that moment it struck Ted what he was dealing with here. The first order of business, however, was to get her warmed up and feeling safe. "Let's go get that coffee, Lisa. Okay?"

She nodded. He offered his hand to help her up. She started to stand but the first purchase of weight on her legs produced a sharp scream. She collapsed back down in a litany of pain. "Ow, ow, ow...Why does it hurt? Why does it hurt?"

"Where?"

"Down...there."

"Okay," Ted said softly. "We'll call you a cab, darlin'."
He hiked up his sweats, bent at the knees, and slid his
forearms under her slender torso. She protested at first
but once he had her weight off the ground, she slipped
her arms around his neck. It was a hundred yards or more
back to the bar, over rough and swampy terrain but he
took it slowly and his footing was sure.

"Lisa," he said when the third cup of coffee seemed to
be having the desired effect, "are you feeling better?"

"Warmer."

He pointed over the bar to the dock area. A half dozen
overnighters were tied up there, a few with lovers asleep
on the deck. "Any of those boats look familiar? Did you
come over to the island on any of those boats?"

"I...I don't think so."

"Lisa, did someone do something to you?"

She began to weep again, but this was not a cry for
help in the wilderness. She was out of danger. Now she
was checking her wounds. "I...I think so."

Ted thought she could use some privacy. "I'll be right
back." He warmed up her cup from the pot, adding a dol-
lop of Irish whiskey, before patting her folded hands and
walking away in the direction of the ramp. On the dock
below, he kicked every hull as he went, bellowing, rousing
the dead. "Wake up! Out of bed! Who knows Lisa Chin?
Who brought Lisa Chin over from the mainland? Wake
up!"

But none of them had brought her. No one knew her.
Ted realized what he had to do next. He didn't want to
upset Lisa so he asked one of the guys if he could use the
VHF aboard his boat to make the call.

Deev's patrol boat pulled into the island about ninety
minutes later. In that time Ted had managed to get Lisa
to eat something solid and then lie down on one of the
chaise mats, covered with a blanket. He told her he'd

14

called the police and she thanked him before falling asleep. Deev brought someone along with him, an officer he introduced as Sergeant Annette Lawrence. She was in her mid-thirties, direct but not harsh, with a very athletic, even muscular build. "Annette is our trauma specialist," Deev explained.

"You're still of the opinion that she was raped?" Annette asked Ted, looking right at him, unblinking. She had gray-hazel eyes.

"I'm no expert," Ted replied, his eyes locked by hers in a curious, unanticipated intensity. "But she says she hurts. And this whole thing about not remembering, it sounds like...you know...rufie."

"Rohypnol? Have you had any trouble with that out here?"

"No, but I read about it." There was a measurable pause as they continued to study each other. Was this suspicion on her part? "Do you want me to wake her up?" Ted offered.

"No, I'll do that," Annette replied.

She walked over to the mat, sat on the ground next to Lisa and gently shook her awake. Ted swung the hinged section up and took his station behind the bar. A fresh pot of coffee was ready. He gave Deev a cup.

"What is this? Am I a suspect?"

Deev smiled. "No, hell no, Teddy. That's just Annette. She's ferocious on these rape cases. But she's okay. She's not one of these 'all men are animals' types. Even though the stuff she sees..." Deev didn't finish his assessment of mankind, preferring to sip his coffee.

"I thought I knew all you guys."

"She's only been with us for six months."

"Married?"

Deev grinned. "No, Ted, but probably not a Spear Island kind of girl." Deev fished his waterproof notebook out of a back pocket and flipped it open to a blank page. "So tell me," he said.

Ted ran it all by Deev, how he had heard the crying, how he had warmed her up, how he had checked the boats at the dock.

"None of them knew her, huh?"

"Or they wouldn't cop to it."

"The truth of it probably is: she came out with a group of guys, somebody gave her the drug, raped her, and left her here. Any idea who that might be?"

"Deev, you've seen it here on a busy night. I can't follow the action. I don't have a clue."

"Okay."

After a few seconds: "There is one possibility."

"Shoot."

"There's a guy who's been running an informal ferry. Picks girls up at Rinaker's and brings them over. Takes them back too, but I'm sure not all of them go back, you know what I mean."

"What's his name?"

"I don't know. I've never seen him, up close. Look, I'm not saying he did this…

"No, no…"

"And I wouldn't want to get him in trouble."

"What kind of trouble?"

"No ferry license, something like that."

"Is he charging a fare?"

"No."

"Then he doesn't need a license. But he does sound like someone I should talk to."

"He'll be here tonight. Pulls in about nine."

Their attention was drawn to the dock. Annette was helping Lisa walk the short distance to the police launch. Deev flipped his notebook shut. "Okay, I'll be back."

Deev jogged down the ramp and joined Annette as they got Lisa situated comfortably in the stern seat. Deev fired up the outboard and was just ready to cast off when Annette spoke to him. He idled back on the engines. Annette got off the boat and came up the dock toward the bar. Ted knew she was coming to talk to him again and he braced himself.

But her manner was quite different. Even the color of her eyes was changed, more green and less gray. "Lisa asked me to thank you."

"No problem."

"From talking to her, I think you're right. About Rohypnol. You did exactly the right thing with her."

"Good."

"She said you carried her, is that right?"

Ted nodded.

"Okay. Thank you for your help, Mr. Kirkpatrik."

She gave him a small but warm smile, then turned and strode with purpose back to the launch. Ted watched them depart for the River Police substation upriver and smiled to himself.

As promised, Deev returned about dusk that night. And, as predicted, soon after dark the ferry arrived at Spear Island to land a group of young women. As busy as he was at the pump, Ted kept an eye on the developments. Deev approached the Ferryman and was invited aboard. They sat in the stern for five minutes, no more, Deev making notes in his pad. At one point he showed the ferryman a photograph. Before he disembarked, Deev put the boat through an equipment inspection. From various lazarettes and hatches, the Ferryman produced a half dozen life vests, a first aid kit, a fire extinguisher, a fog horn, a radar reflector, a toolbox. He demonstrated a high-powered searchlight. Ted had seen Deev put dozens of boats through this test. The Ferryman passed. He stowed the gear again, then departed, to float aimlessly in the channel, to do whatever he did before returning in the wee hours to complete the round trip.

Deev came up the ramp and approached the mobbed bar. "Hey, buddy," Ted whispered to a kid who looked illegal, "do me a favor and let the police officer sit down for a minute?"

The barstool cleared and Deev sat. "So, does he know anything?"

"No. He never saw her before."

"She wasn't one of his girls?"

"He said no."

"Seem like he's telling the truth?"

"I believe him."

"Why does he do it?"

"I don't think he did anything…"

"No, I mean, why does he run that ferry?"

"I didn't ask him that, Ted."

"Why not?"

"It's his enterprise. So long is it's not illegal, it's none of my business. Or yours."

"What's his name?"

"Why do you need to know that?"

"Come on, Deev, this isn't the CIA."

Deev sighed, opened his notebook and turned it around so Ted could read it. There was a name, an ordinary name, nothing special, with the name of a town written beneath.

Ted tapped the name of the town. "Where's that?"

"New York. Long Island. His driver's license was less than a year old, so I asked."

"He moves all the way across the country to ferry people across a river, for free? Doesn't that make you wonder?"

"Hell, Ted, I don't know. In the great scheme of things, I worry more about Rohypnol than gypsy ferries. Does he cause you any trouble? Isn't he bringing business your way? I wonder why *you* wonder."

Two weekends later, Ted noticed something out of the corner of his eye.

In his ten years on Spear, Ted had seen every sleight of hand gag that human evolution had produced. He'd seen a hundred cool ways to light a cigarette, six dozen where's-the-coin tricks. He seen every way there was to burn a toothpick down to the edge of a glass. He'd seen every variety of the shell game, of Three-card Monty and Follow the Queen. He'd seen some very slick poaching: money lifted, cigarettes gone missing, keys pocketed, phone numbers misdirected. He'd seen broken finger gags, missing finger gags, jackknife between the knuckles gags, double-jointed gags, cat's cradle gags, and how many times had he opened the door to see all the people and gotten the finger instead?

This was different. It was Saturday night and the band was in the middle of one of its rave numbers, an extended instrumental frenzy. He couldn't see the dance floor but there must have been some hot exhibition going on because every face was turned away from him. At the end of the bar, a tall guy had his arm around a girl. Ted watched as his arm dropped to a cigarette pack at the bar. But instead of a cigarette, he withdrew a small glass vial. With a dexterity that suggested practice, he popped the plastic cap off the vial and emptied the powdered contents into the girl's tumbler of rum punch. Without looking, he replaced the vial and stirred it into her drink with her own straw.

They were just turning back to drink when Ted got there. He swiped both glasses away from them. "Hey, what're you doing, man?" came the protest.

"The fruit gets nasty near the bottom of the barrel. I'll change the batch and get you fresh."

"We wanted those."

Ted ignored him and collected glasses from the vial guy's two buddies. "Let me have 'em, guys. Fresh ones coming up."

"You can't just take somebody's drink without asking. I want it back," the tall guy snarled.

In deliberate full view, Ted poured the tainted glass down the sink. "Spilled milk, pal," he said coolly.

"Asshole!"

"I do you a favor and you call me names?"

"Fuck you."

"Now that's really immature. I wonder if you're even old enough to be in here. Let me see some ID."

"Leave him alone," one of the other guys said.

"Yours too," Ted replied. He pointed to each one in turn. "All of you."

"We showed 'em to that fat Arab at the door."

Ted raised his voice more than a notch. "ID on the table! Now!"

The bar was silenced. The girl slid off her stool and melted away, wanting no part of this. Yosef drifted up soundlessly to grasp her vacant stool with massive hands. "Trouble, Ted?" he asked in a flat voice.

"Is this the fat Arab you were talking about?" Ted asked.

Slowly, wallets came out of back pockets and licenses hit the bar. All laminated, all California. Ted picked them up, studying one in particular. He held the document up next to the tall guy's face. "Big for fourteen."

"I'm twenty-fucking-four."

"No, you're bounced. Off the island, now!"

The tall guy was about to respond when Yosef dragged him off the stool, smoothly and directly into a wrestling hold which looked both painful and inescapable. Hoots of approval from the rest of the bar.

"And take your twelve-year-old friends with you."

A welter of derision followed them as Yosef helped them find their vessel and assisted their departure.

After that, the night wound down without further incident. The Ferryman came and collected his passengers with a single toot on the air horn. Ted cleaned up and waited for Deev to come and check that the island had cleared. Deev never showed but that had happened before. Nothing left to do but walk the long, narrow float dock to his "residence" and crash hard.

A light hit him and he knew it was not dawn. Sunrise was a muted, murky affair on the Delta. This was a bolt from the blue, filling up the "Residence" with blinding incandescent clarity. Ted stumbled on deck. The light was coming from the channel but as soon as it had his attention, it moved off along the dock to intersect with young guys approaching in a single file. They were the same three guys Ted had booted from the island earlier. Two carried fish clubs, one a gaff hook.

When he caught sight of the outrage coming for him, Ted involuntarily wet his pants. But the would-be assailants also lost it when the light hit them. The sort of work they had planned was best done in the dark and they suddenly looked like bathing beauties caught naked. "Fuck!" They turned and stumbled over each other to get back to their boat and shove off. One dropped his aluminum club into the channel. The light followed them until they were clearly back in the river channel and headed away.

Ted, still shaking and sweaty in his "60-30's," came out onto the dock. The light swung back to him once more before its power was cut. In the debilitating after-image, Ted could not see a thing but he knew who deserved his gratitude.

"Thanks, Deev."

There was silence across the water. Ted strained to get his eyes to work; the world remained a tracery of persistent capillaries.

"Deev? I owe you one."

No answer except the sound of an engine cranking up and then fading away in the direction of the main channel.

Every Sunday in the summer months the Hungarian would arrive in his boat and take away the week's receipts. The cash was kept in a hidden safe in a wall of the outhouse, the most permanent building on the island. He was quite pleased with the way the summer was running, the best revenues ever. Was there a particular reason? Was it the pirate ship motif? Yes, Ted could think of no other reason for the upturn.

While the Hungarian and his extended family made the count, Ted asked if he could borrow his boss's cell phone to make a private call.

First he called Deev's home number but there was no answer. Then he tried the non-emergency number.

"Stockton Police Department."

"Officer Devareau, please."

"I'm sorry, Officer Devareau is away on a three-day leave."

"He is?"

"Is there anyone else who can help you?"

"Uh, okay, um...Sergeant Lawrence?"

"She's not on duty today. Can I take a number?"

"Well, I'm kind of hard to reach. This is Ted Kirkpatrik calling from Spear Island..."

"Oh, yes, Mr. Kirkpatrik. Annette said to give you her home number if you called."

"She did?"

A minute later he was on the line with Annette Lawrence. Her voice sounded quite different, softer, even dreamy. She admitted to being in the middle of the Chronicle in the middle of a lazy Sunday.

"How is Lisa?" Ted asked.

"Much better. I say that despite the fact that she's certain now she was raped."

"Did she remember how she got over here?"

"Yeah, with a friend of her cousin. They thought she went back on another boat."

"That happens a lot."

"I'll admit I'm kind of stuck on this case."

"Well, let me tell you what happened here last night." He told her about the incident at the bar. "It was clear from his reaction, I was screwing up some major plan for the evening. I got it just before she drank."

"I'll arrange for one of the patrol guys to pick it up."

"What?"

"The drink."

"The drink? No, I threw it out."

"You threw it out?"

"Damn. I'm sorry. That was really stupid. But the way it happened, I sort of had to."

"That's okay. I'm sure you had no choice."

"You want his address?"

"How did you get his address?"

"I carded him."

Annette laughed. He could hear the delight in her voice even over the Hungarian's cut-rate cell. "Now that's detective work. And yes, I would love to pay this guy a personal visit."

Ted gave her the full name and address.

"If something develops out of this, I may need you to come in and pick this fellow out of a line-up. Testify at the trial, too."

"I can do that."

"Do you come into town often?"

"Hardly ever in the season."

"Well, at least that's one island where you won't get lonely."

"Don't be too sure about that." There was a moment of silence between them. "Uh, Sergeant...They told me when I called the office that Bill Devareau was on leave."

"He and his boy went fishing, up in the Sierras."

"When did he leave?"

"Two days ago."

"Who was working my section of the river last night, do you know?"

"I don't, offhand. I can find out."

"I'd appreciate that."

"Got a complaint?"

"Just the opposite. Well...Bye."

"Bye."

He closed the phone slowly. There had been a certain warmth in that last exchange: "Bye." "Bye." He shook it off. He was perfectly capable of reading in too much when it came to women. He had trained himself to discount their across-the-bar intimacies; they were intimate *because* the bar was there and Annette Lawrence was on the safe side of a much wider bar. Still....

The Hungarian and his family departed with a suitcase full of greenbacks about four in the afternoon. Even as they were leaving the air had turned colder and clouds had begun to well up in the northwestern sky. By Sunday night it was raining straight across in a high gale.

It was an unusual summer storm. Blame it on *el Niño*. The mainland disappeared from sight in a welter of rain and driven spray. He contacted Yosef and told him Spear was closed until the storm passed.

His only guests were on Tuesday, three guys off a large chartered cruiser which had to battle its way across the swollen river into the Spear Island inlet. These guys were desperate. They had spent two days at anchor behind White's Point waiting out the storm and had drunk all their beer and smoked every shred of tobacco. Once the cigarettes had run out, one of them had been selling the others drags on a cheap cigar for one dollar a draw. Their mood was ugly and Ted took pity on them. He got them filled with rum and sold them a carton of Marlboro right out of the storehouse. Levels of alcohol and nicotine stabilized.

"From New York?" Ted asked even though their accents made the question unnecessary.

"We are," said the cigar smoker. "He lives on the island."

"Long Island?"

"Yeah, Long Island. Something wrong with that?"

"I don't know, you tell me." No reply. "You know a town called...uh..." Ted thought a half second, then remembered the name that Deev had shown him.

"Yeah, I know it."

"What's it like?"

"Nothing special."

Cigar Smoker disagreed. "Whatchu talking about? That's where that plane blew up."

"Oh, yeah, that's right."

"Are you talking about the Paris plane?" Ted asked.

"Yeah. What a fucking mess."

"They were piling up bodies there for weeks."

"Tragedy is, it was shot down by our own Navy."

"Oh, please…"

"Here we go again…"

"There is this flash of light climbing over the ocean. *Climbing*, asshole. That means a missile."

"That means you spend way too much time on the Internet."

Once they left, Ted was alone in the rain. He spent a few lazy days lying on his back in the Residence, catching up on his sleep, thinking over the events of his last summer. It hadn't gone the way he'd thought. Things had surprised him: the tenderness he'd felt toward the victim, Lisa Chin. His piss-pants fear as those guys crept toward him on the dock. His cautious curiosity about Annette Lawrence. And the Ferryman.

The storm passed and the island roared for the next couple of weeks. Ted pulled the pump handle a thousand times an hour and the partying crowd was brightened nearly every night by a boatload of Rinaker's Landing girls. It was turning into the least raucous, least brutal, most convivial summer he could remember. Yosef had broken up a grand total of two fights.

Deev returned from his rained-out fishing vacation, but he had no idea who should get credit for saving Ted's ass. He did have a message for Ted, however: Sergeant

Lawrence was making progress with the Chin rape case. She wanted him to come in on Friday and pick someone out of a line-up.

"I think she's interested in you," Deev added with a mischievous smile. "Sees you as some kind of free-wheeling Island King."

"You'll set her straight."

"You mean, tell her the truth about you? I would, if I knew it."

Ted felt suddenly uncomfortable with the prospect of the trip across the water. Normally he would hitch a ride across the back bayou with Henri and Ulysses on their supply barge, but this time... "Uh, Deev, can I ask a favor?"

"Sure, Ted."

"Can I get a ride back with you late tonight?"

"No problem."

"Can I...like...take a shower at your house?"

"Yeah."

"How about me doing some laundry? So I'll have something clean to wear?"

"Sure: Laundry, shower, sleep on the sofa. Got to look good when you go a-courting."

"You're such a troublemaker. How'd you get a badge?"

Deev flicked his tin. "Six box-tops."

He'd never met Deev's wife or son and he didn't meet them this time, either. They were asleep when Ted and Deev got there and long gone from the house by the time they woke up. Ted hung around in one of Deev's bathrobes as the washer and dryer, in one big load each, restored his wardrobe. About three in the afternoon, they rode into district headquarters.

Annette was waiting for Ted in the lobby. She exceeded Ted's memory of her, from the one time they had met in person. She was wearing the very same uniform and carried about her the same serious devotion to duty, but he felt an undercurrent. Deev said she was interested in him. It had been a long time since something like that had happened. He had spent a sleepless night on Deev's sofa trying to remember how to move it to the next level, but cheap Spear Island pick-up lines were all he could recall. Had he been running the pump too many years to be sincere? He'd just have to find the moment and say what came to mind.

She clearly enjoyed showing him around her workplace: the communications center, the computer center, the fingerprint center.

"The doughnut center," Ted teased as they passed a lunch area.

"Shall we have one?"

As they ate, she brought him up to date on their case. "I had a long talk with Mr. Phil Hargood," she said. Phil Hargood was the guy Ted had caught with the vial. "He admitted being on Spear Island the night the Lisa was attacked but that was all."

"What about the other night?"

"He said you singled him out for no reason and had him thrown off the island."

"What else is he going to say?"

"No, it's what you'd expect. If we could get a DNA sample from him, we might match it to hair and semen we found on Lisa. But he's not cooperating. I hope a judge can be convinced to issue an order, on the basis of what you saw."

A uniformed officer came into the snack room and announced to Sergeant Lawrence that her line-up was ready. She led Ted down a corridor to a small dark room on the end. There was a slab of one-way glass and four guys in the next room. "Do you recognize him in this group?" Lawrence asked.

"Right there," Ted pointed to Hargood. "On the left end."

"You are certain?"

"Oh, yeah."

"Will you say so in court?"

"With my hand on a Bible."

She spoke into an intercom and told the line-up that it was dismissed.

"I'm impressed," Ted offered sincerely. "You really know this stuff. You really go after these guys."

"Well, you make a little progress. There's a lot more bad than good, it seems like."

"That's been my impression, too."

The light from the line-up room snapped off, leaving them in semi-darkness. Ted felt a quickening of sudden intimacy. "But you get surprised now and then," he offered in a whisper.

She said nothing. Ted could barely see her. He was hesitant but there would never be a time like this again.

"Annette," he started...

"Mister Kirkpatrik," she said at the same instant. "I'm sorry?"

"No, no, please, what were you going to say?"

"Would you do one more thing for me? Since you're here."

"Sure."

"I'd like a sample of your blood."

"My blood?"

"Your DNA."

Ninety minutes later Ted was walking somewhere. He thought it was the general direction of Deev's house but he wasn't sure and he didn't care. She had wanted a sample of his DNA. It was too bitter a thing.

Oh, she'd recited every excuse and disclaimer in the Detective Sergeants' Handbook. She was not, of course, after him for the crime against Lisa. It was just standard procedure to collect these samples. If they ever went to trial against Hargood, the defense couldn't divert suspicion to Ted as an untested suspect. And if they found samples on Lisa that matched him, they could eliminate those, figuring she'd gotten them when he very kindly carried her from the site of the crime.

It was bullshit. He could hear it in her voice. What had Deev said—she was interested in him? More than interested. She suspected. She thought it possible that he had drugged and raped the girl. That he had pretended to find Lisa and care about her welfare. That he had tried to divert suspicion, first to the Ferryman, then to Hargood. She saw him as some kind of fevered pervert, a degenerate. Ted felt sour to the core. What a laugh. Suppose he had gotten around to saying those words, asked her out on a date? "Sure, Ted, I'll go to the movies with you. But first, can we find a vein?"

This was his last summer. He'd said it. He was going to give the Hungarian notice and never come back. He was going to live in a nicer world, off Spear Island. But the nice world wanted him to stay out there. With the rogue asparagus. The nice world wanted nothing to do with him. It only wanted his blood, to fix his place in a textbook display of misfits.

"Fuck her," he said out loud. It felt good, but where did that leave him? Fuck her? Fuck everyone who comes to the island? Fuck everyone who doesn't? Who's fucking left, Ted?

He was walking along a series of old docks that lined a limpid backwater of the San Joaquin. Through his poisonous internal monologue, he just barely heard the sound of a boat's engine approaching. When he looked up he saw a Bayliner gliding by alongside.

"Mister Kirkpatrik?"

Ted was not surprised he knew his name. Everybody knew Ted the Pump.

"Do you want a ride over?"

Ted stopped and looked. It was the first time he'd seen him close up in sunlight. The Ferryman gazed back at him with a pair of copper-green eyes. He was in his late twenties, perhaps a little older. There was a strength in his long and vaguely Scandinavian face, a certain stay-the-course determination despite its unweathered texture. Ted had a flash of intuition—this man once wore a uniform. Navy. Coast Guard or police. He just had the gravity.

"I thought you only took girls," Ted replied.

"I don't take men at night. But I can take you now."

Ted simply nodded. He swung a leg over the gunwale and sat in the bow. The Ferryman swung the stern out into the channel and then went slow ahead. They were in a "No Wake" zone. It was strange. All summer Ted had thought about this guy and what he would say if he got the chance. Now he had nothing to ask. So he sat in painful, ruminative silence all the way out to the river. Once the boat arrived in the main channel and the Ferryman throttled her up to speed, there was no way to talk over the engine's whine anyway. Ted looked ahead, toward the island home he deserved. The few times he glanced back, he could see the Ferryman's isolating concentration: "I'm sorry, I need to pay attention to the river."

They were in mid-channel, current and wind both running against them, when the boat suddenly shrugged off its mantle of speed and wallowed as the world's water overtook the stern. The Ferryman spun the wheel and the boat turned 180 degrees into its own frothing history.

They pitched and rolled in the confused surface geometry. Ted looked around and saw the man handing him a small white box.

"You're bleeding," said the Ferryman.

Ted looked down at his right arm just below the inner elbow. His arms were thick and tough; it had taken the medical technician four tries to find a vein. He had ripped off the sterile pad in a rage. "I know," Ted replied.

"Band-Aids in here."

"They won't help. This is a lethal wound."

The Ferryman's eyes, the color of copper verdigris, held Ted square in their gaze. "You think you're going to die from that?"

"Yes."

"You won't."

"How do you know?"

"I know...what it takes to make someone dead."

"There's all kinds of dead."

"No, just one. Everything else is a mood."

The Ferryman placed the First Aid kit on a bulkhead. Just to the right of it, a quartz/halogen searchlight was mounted. Ted glanced at it and the Ferryman did too. A realization.

"That was you."

The Ferryman said nothing.

"You know what I'm talking about. That night on my dock. *You* put the light on those guys. This light. Didn't you? Didn't you? Look, I want to thank you. I'm not angry."

"You sound angry."

"I'm not. I mean, I am...but not about that. I'm just saying thank you, if you did it. Is it okay to say thank you? The girls? They say thank you, when you bring them back and forth."

The Ferryman nodded.

"So, thank you." There was a silence between them. "Why do you do these things? Is that it? Just for the gratitude?"

The Ferryman said nothing.

"Look, I really want to know."

"Why ask?"

"It's important to me. Why do you do this?"

The Ferryman stared past Ted, over the bow, looking east. "No reason. Just...I can tell at some distance who needs help...and who is beyond needing it."

"You made a mistake today."

"No," said the Ferryman. "I did not. You'll live."

The next moment, the throttles went forward, the acceleration pressed Ted into his seat. And into himself. It took them only minutes to make Spear Island Inlet at that speed and, by the time they got there, Ted found he had left Annette and her suspicions behind. He watched his home appear around the big bend in the San Joaquin. He had always taken the supply barge over. Not once had he viewed it from this perspective, arriving on the river on a sunny day, as the rest of the world saw it. He caught sight of Henri and Ulysses' ridiculous pirate ship and found himself laughing out loud. It was so huge and playful and crazy. Was it really any mystery why his customers got playful and crazy when they landed? There was the bar and there was the pump. He never realized people could see him from this far away. What was it Deev had called him, a "free-wheeling Island King?" Well, maybe that's what he was, and why the fuck not?

The Bayliner kissed Spear Island dock at the end of a perfect approach and Ted stepped ashore. "Thanks," he said. He reached for his wallet. "I must owe you something."

"No charge," said the Ferryman.

TOGGLESMOOCH

a post-feminist fable

The Bayou Anglais is dark here in the main channel, the dark tannin tea of the swamp. The bottomless color spreads bank to bank. But we travel upwater and soon it will begin to clear, become a brown, become a green. In an hour or less, if my old outboard holds up and if no one waves me over to share a smoke and talk, I will turn up one of the little creeks which feed the Bayou. I have one in mind. There the water runs near clean and in the shallows one can see bottom. We will go on the pole then and float deep into the wilderness. When my skiff puts her nose on the farthest mud bar, if there are no snakes to be seen around, there is where I will put you over the side, John Surrey, watch you sink, and leave you forever.

I hope you understand. I think you do.

My Elizabeth must have been beautiful that summer five years ago. Her hair would have been solid black and her slender body even more desirable as she slept naked under the mosquito net of her tent. Ah, I can dream…

And the irony is she had been so near to me, physically that is, on her small island in the Great Louisiana swamp. She was only a few miles away, but I did not know her yet.

Actually, she had come to the swamp three summers in a row, to fulfill her research as a herpetologist. The days had been spent capturing and studying frogs, salamanders and some little snakes. But it was not all work. Near the end of the summer two of her friends from the university rented a boat and made an annual voyage to her island, to stay overnight for what we Cajun call a *fais do-do*. A get-together. A do.

Elizabeth fried up the catfish filets and they talked. You can imagine, *mes amis*: three women, professors or near-professors at the same college? They had a lot of talking to do, about work, the state of the world, university politics. Over coffee, Dr. Mendelssohn dug out the liter of cheap brandy she had brought from the mainland and they finally got down to talking about the ultimate topic. What we Cajun call *les liaisons*. What they called "relationships."

Dr. Mendelssohn had lived through a bad summer. The promising gentleman of June had become the pig of August. "But I thought he was more evolved than that," Dr. Raymond offered in sympathy.

"So did I. He said all the right things. He tickled all the right spots."

"He knew where the spots were, that's to his credit."

"Oh, they're not un-clever, as a race. They learn what we want, what we want to hear. But it's just a veneer, friends."

"George?" my Elizabeth asked. "Are we talking about the same George?"

"George to you and me. To his buddies he's 'G'. As in 'Yo, G, you still fucking that professor bitch?'"

"No!"

"Direct quote. To which he answered: 'Yeah, still tapping it.'"

"I don't believe it." My Elizabeth always thought the best of people.

"I believe it," said Dr. Mendelssohn. "I swear, there's not a one of them who can rise above the indoctrination of centuries."

"It's not indoctrinary," clarified Dr. Raymond, a historian. "It's genetic."

"It's only partly genetic," Mendelssohn, the psychologist, disputed.

"The old argument," Elizabeth observed.

"Yes…."

They passed the brandy around the fire once, silently thinking. "It would be an interesting experiment."

"What experiment?"

"Give me a male of the species no more than five years old…"

"Cradle robber."

"No, I'm serious. A boy child, born into a neutral environment…"

"Where do you find that? Mars?"

"…Monitor his hormonal balance…"

"In men? No such thing."

"…And see if it's possible."

"To nurture the nature out of him?"

"The drum-pounders would lynch you for such talk."

"What you are describing," Elizabeth observed, "is parenthood."

"Let's not get carried away."

Perhaps you overheard this conversation, watching and waiting. Perhaps not. I will tell the story anyway. We still have far to go.

They talked late into the night, as the sounds of the swamp grew thicker and closer to the fire. They drew closer, too. They hugged. They were sisters. But when the bottle of brandy and the fire were low, there was a *passer d'ange*. A moment of silence, of lingering despair.

"It's all just impossible."

"I know."

"I used to have hope. Now...I don't think I'll never find the one."

"I don't need Prince Charming, just someone who's a tiny bit charming."

"Duke Charming."

"Fuck it–Sergeant Charming."

"I'd settle for that."

The brandy had gone to my Elizabeth's head more than the others'. Where it had made them sad, it made her full of mischief. She got up and staggered over to where her beloved subjects were held securely in small cages, high off the ground from the snakes. When she returned to the firelight she carried a small common green.

"*Rana clamitans*," she announced as she dropped him in Dr. Mendelssohn's lap. "Take a chance, Susie. Why settle for a Count when the swamp is full of Princes?"

Laughing, they passed the frightened froggie hand to hand. Each of them puckered up and gave him a great smooch on his grim, sealed lips.

"You can do better than that!"

"Don't be shy, My Prince."

"It isn't working, Liz."

"Maybe you have to French kiss."

"Ew..."

"Think of the <u>tongue</u>!"

Soon after this, they crept into the tent, unrolled their sleeping bags, laughed a last time and said good night. Elizabeth loved her friends but she was not so despairing as they. Men were not alien to her. She had simply not yet found the special one. There was no you, there was no me. These were her thoughts as she surrendered to the hollow, dreamless sleep of brandy.

When her friends departed at mid-morning the next day, Elizabeth waved to them until their skiff rounded the bend in the river, then groped back to her tent and collapsed again, head and stomach dancing together.

She awoke with a heavy sensation in her chest. She looked up to find it was not in her chest but on it. A huge American Bullfrog, *Rana catesbeiana*, truly the largest she had ever seen, was perched smugly between her breasts, calmly observing her amazed face.

She saw the tent flap, which she had failed to close. "Hello," she greeted it and slowly sat up. The frog transferred to her lap, unafraid, in fact quite content. He was a true beauty with enormous eyes and a powerful spine and legs. His underbelly was the smoothest milky white. Each fine finger and toe was marvelously detailed. And on his back, markings of a kind she had never seen before: sensuous, elongated lozenges, flush full in the middle and tapering at the ends, like a pair of lips concealing the merest Mona Lisa smile.

"Aren't you a beauty?" She held him up to her face. The frog inched closer. His amphibian's eyelids squeezed open and closed hypnotically.

"You should have been here last night," Elizabeth whispered. "Three on one, a froggie's dream." She brought her lips to his and kissed him.

There was a rapturous noise. A stunning musical chord filled the tent, the camp, the swamp. Loud it was, like the shriek of the *chemin de fer*, yet not one bird rose from its branch in fear, not a single fish wriggled down to the mute safety of the depths. Then, immediately, the resonance cleared like a morning fog. She screamed. A naked man was with her in the tent, squatting on oversized haunches, staring at her with grateful, somewhat enlarged eyes.

"Thank you," he said.

My Elizabeth found her voice. "Who...who are you?"

"I....I don't know, exactly," the man said slowly. "But I belong to you."

"People don't own people."

"Really? I seem to remember that they did."

"I do not believe this. How did you get here?"

"You brought me back."

"I did not. I just..." She stopped. No. She would not accept that. She turned instead to the matter at hand. "Get out of here."

The man looked profoundly distressed and saddened by her request. His voice grew small, like a chastised toddler's. "You want me to leave?"

My Elizabeth saw the hurt in his eyes. "I mean...get out of the tent, at least. And get some clothes on. In my pack, hanging on the tree."

The man's face became incandescent with joy. She had never met anyone whose emotions were more transparent. "I will get them. I will put them on. I belong to you."

"Stop saying that!" she cried, but the man was gone already, bolting from the tent like a big bony puppy. He took the pole and guy lines with him and the heavy canvas settled over my Elizabeth like an oath of office.

You do not look left or right. I have your undivided attention. That is good, because you must know all of this story to understand what will happen to you when we reach the place.

How do I know all of this, you might ask. My Elizabeth told me much herself, of course. Also, soon after she found the man, she started keeping a *journal*, a daily book.

She has permitted me to read it. Like her, the book began as one thing and became slowly another.

Like her, the book intended at first to study the phenomenal man. With such a discovery in hand, there could be no thought of completing the summer's research. That day, my Elizabeth struck her island camp and took the man back to the university. "Carsick the whole way," she wrote.

It was easy to keep him a secret, at least at first. The campus was quiet in those last two weeks of the summer and she lived alone in small house that was isolated at the end of a leafy cul-de-sac. It had a garden enclosed by a high brick wall. The man loved her garden. He would sit out in the haze of full summer afternoons, and in the evening he would watch the fireflies. My Elizabeth observed him carefully. Her journal was bursting with theories: parallel universe, flash-bang evolution, animistic magic. The man seemed to resist inquiry. No, wait, that's not what she said. He would always answer her questions, but his answers....

"I am not who I wish to be," he said.

"Hopper stopper," he said.

"Hopper chopper."

What did it mean?

Her discipline drove her on. "Now, I want to know. I want a straight answer."

"There is the place made of water and the place made of...Elizabeth."

Over the arch of those balmy days, the sternness of inquiry melted from her. She never got out the camera or the calipers. They would head into the garden and sit together on the verdant late-summer grass, and before she knew it, dusk was upon them. It was like a spell.

Then, suddenly, the spell was broken; she learned the terrible secret. It was illness that scattered the trance: a rainstorm chill, followed by a sleepless night into which a fever marched unopposed. He was helpless and it gobbled him up. I see my poor Elizabeth, posted at the man's bedside as his fever spiraled up and up, pouring her worst fears into the pages of her book: "His eyes have retreated into themselves. The second night of thunder is here and I feel so powerless."

"I will be right here," she whispered to soothe him. "I will not leave." She stroked his damp black hair from his strong face. It felt fine and aristocratic between her fingers. From the depth of his fever, he seemed to feel her touch and take some comfort. She bent over and kissed his perspiring brow.

There was a faint cluster of tones. It was a thousand times more delicate than before but she recognized the harmonics at once. On the damp pillow below sat the Great American Bullfrog.

She fell back with a gasp. She regained her composure, snatched it up and kissed it hard on the nose. A chord… and the man was back. He was cooler to the touch. He opened his eyes and smiled. My Elizabeth kissed him again, to make frog, then again, to make man. Her eyes were wide with revelation. "Binary," she whispered.

"What?" said the man.

"You toggle."

"I do feel much better, thank you."

"I think I can cure you altogether."

She left him amphibian for a solid thirty minutes this time, her heart racing with anxiety the whole period. What if she were wrong, or what if there were some kind of minimum cycle? But the instant her lips brushed his, he toggled back to humanity, fever banished. "Can we go into the garden?"

"I think you'd better stay in bed a while."

"Whatever you say, Elizabeth. I belong to you."

Campus began filling up, her students and colleagues returning, so it became imperative that she give him an identity. He became John Surrey, of England, a distant cousin who had spent his formative years in the Falkland Islands. This explained his vaguely British accent and his unfamiliarity with things worldly and modern. Then she used her influence with the university to enroll him in some basic Community Extension classes: English, American History, and Introduction to Biology. John Surrey had no sense of history but enjoyed that class the most.

He could read perfectly well and wrote rather beautifully. Years later, my Elizabeth showed me some of the letters and poems that came home in a schoolboy's notebook. Always, she was the subject. "I guess he has a little bit of a crush on me," she told the inquiring English teacher. "Very good," is what she told John. He was delighted with any praise but she felt hollow in giving it. His words deserved more but, at that time, she feared what the more was.

As for his toggling, this they explored in greater detail. He trusted her implicitly and gave himself to the other side whenever she wished. They discovered that a proper kiss was not necessary. Any contact of her lips to his skin, the merest swipe, an accidental brushing even on nails or hair sent John toggling back and forth. And as for the strange music that accompanied the change, it put my Elizabeth in mind of a boy she had once lived with in her college days, a wild-ass musician who had made an elated exclamation while under a potent dose of LSD: "Liz, Liz, I heard it! I heard the Big Note."

Elizabeth suspected that what she heard with John Surrey was that same Big Note.

She realized the enormous responsibility she held, but that didn't mean they could not have some fun. John loved the movies and became a great fan of amusement park rides. There was many a turnstile that John Surrey finessed, hunkered down next to checkbook and keys in the bottom of Elizabeth's purse. Indeed, he felt very happy there, among those other things which belonged to her.

Of course, it was all a little patronizing, wasn't it? He adored her, he owed everything to her, and she held enormous power over him. John Surrey was a living fairy tale, an unreal changeling who still cried out "Hopper chopper" in his sleep. Not entirely human. But also, not an object. In honest moments of reflection, my righteous Elizabeth had to ask the question: Isn't this the way men treat women?

If so, what had she become?

"My God, Liz, he's wonderful!"

"A Falkland Islander?"

"I know where I'm taking my next vacation."

"And such devotion to you, you must feel just wonderful."

"What does he mean when he says he belongs to you?" Dr. Raymond asked. Gloria worried Elizabeth the most, as far as John was concerned. She was a beauty with well-established appetites.

"It's...just how he speaks," Elizabeth explained.

"Does he date?"

"I don't think he's ready, yet."

"What do you mean, 'ready'?"

"For American girls. He still has a lot to learn." She threw an accusatory gaze at Gloria. "His biology course hasn't gotten to the section on predators yet."

"*Touché.*"

Still, her heart nearly vaulted from her chest as Gloria stopped at the door and, before Liz could intervene, pecked John on the cheek. My Elizabeth grimaced, poised for the Big Note, which would signal his toggling and the end of their secret.

The horrible moment passed. There stood John, still pink and human, waving good-bye to Gloria. Gloria's kiss had had no effect. My Elizabeth was very relieved. Or was she?

It was this uncertainty which lead her to change her plans. She was planning to fly to Washington D.C. for a few days for research. Her original idea was to leave John alone in the house as he suffered so from motion sickness. But after her tea with the girls, her own comment about "predators" began to worry her mind and she decided John should go along.

The travel plans were not difficult to change. It only required a large carry-on bag with some saw grass secretively strewn in the bottom. While still in the car in the parking structure, my Elizabeth brought her sweet lips to bear. As John toggled to frog, Elizabeth thought she saw a look of wild hope in his eyes and then realized why: for the first time since the first time, she had kissed him square on the lips. What did that mean? What did he think it meant?

She was so wrapped up in these thoughts that she did not see the man coming. A hard jerk stripped her of her handbag in a single movement. She screamed, but the robber was as swift and sure as the strike of the *serpent vert.* Her heart foundered with paralyzing grief, like a bright new skiff suddenly holed and rapidly filling. Her outcry of loss brought the airport security men.

"A frog?"

"Yes, a big one, an American bullfrog," my Elizabeth said through her tears. "With two funny marks on the back."

"Pretty attached to this animal, are you, Miss?"

"You've got to find him."

"I wouldn't get my hopes up," the men said, but they did explain their procedure. When purse snatching was reported in the airport, they made a special effort to search through the trash bins and dumpsters at the end of the day for stripped and discarded bags. They told her to go home and they would inform her of the results.

My Elizabeth was magnificent; she would not be moved. At day's end, she was the first to pull on the plastic gloves. Down through the newspapers and cigarette packets and soiled paper diapers she rooted. Tooth-scalloped pizza crusts and half moons of rancid coffee in Styrofoam cups. Gray hand towels and yellowed Kleenex and black chicken bones—nothing stopped her.

Then, from deep in the man-made mire, there came a plaintive croak. "John!" she cried. She dove and found you. You were trembling and flattened and covered with shreds of used Kleenex. But in that moment, fortunate one, she loved you.

Washington was forgotten. Back at her house, she placed you in the bathtub and washed you thoroughly, gently, and then summoned John Surrey with a kiss. The Big Note lingered on bathroom tile as her eyes gazed into yours. Her hands were on your body. In a moment, she was in your arms.

Sometime later, in the looping way time passes when one is in the bloom of love, they found the bed and joined again. In the throes of passion, Elizabeth lost herself and her lips went to yours. It was a mistake one can understand and one quickly remedied.

"I'm sorry."

"Do not be sorry."

"I will never be able to kiss you, John."

"We will live without."

And they did, for some measure of time. Alas, *mes amis*, I cannot say happily ever after.

Human nature rides a cruel whip-saw. The contentment of one is the restlessness of another. The heart is never sated with the riches at hand; it fixes always on that which is out of reach. Denial becomes desire; it is a sad curse.

One morning, my Elizabeth awoke to find John Surrey absent from her bed and a frog in his place. With her lips she plucked him back from the other side. "Did I kiss you? In my sleep? I don't remember."

"No, I kissed you."

"Why?"

"I thought maybe...if you were asleep, if you didn't know, it wouldn't work."

"No, darling, it works the same, I'm sorry. You really want to be able to kiss me, don't you? You really miss it."

"No. I mean, yes, but...if I did miss it, what would it matter?" For the first time, wistful sorrow from John Surrey.

His lips were subject to no such leash. He roamed her every part. He wrested answering cries of desire from the only part of her forbidden to him. How she grew to hate her required bedroom pose: the lady of breeding, submitting to the caresses of lowly John Surrey, but always remaining in sufficient command of her senses to keep that chin high and those regal lips out of range.

Noblesse Oblige or the Big Note. It was the Devil's choice.

It was about this time that she finally made the journey to Washington, leaving John Surrey alone for the first time. He was desolated to see her go. Long and with great force they embraced at the garden gate, but of course, their lips could never touch. To both, it seemed a shell of a farewell.

She would have taken him along if her purpose was only research, but there was more. She spent some time there in shadowy company, associating with the kind of men who grow wary at the slightest hint of the unusual, and John Surrey was certainly that. I shudder to think of my Elizabeth in such company, in dark parking lots and low-life taverns, passing over amounts of cash, speaking in codes. But on the airplane back home she felt very proud of her accomplishments, for in her purse was a forged British passport made out in the name of John Surrey. He could now become his own person, able to open a bank account, make a contract, perhaps even (did she think?) take a sacrament. It would help, in time, to erase the lingering guilt my Elizabeth harbored for dominating him. Such things mattered to her. She was very content.

Her contentment vanished the moment she got home.

First were the magazines. There were dozens of them, all over the bed and bureau. Most boasted three X's after the title and every one of those X's was deserved. Elizabeth had seen pornography before; she had served on a committee devoted to exposing its abusive, sexist roots. But she was unaware of the narrow-interest marketing that existed: the subject of John's 'reading' was purely and only lips–women's lips in tight focus, working resolutely on a parade of huge penises. Some were loving, some adoring, some gagging, and all, eventually, festooned with semen. John's collection was devoted entirely to one sex act, the act she could never share with him.

She sat on their bed, layered in his fetish. She was indignant, she was crushed, she felt betrayed and inadequate, all at the same time. But when John walked in the door a few minutes later with Gloria Raymond on his arm, these lesser emotions succumbed to rage.

"You son-of-a-bitch!"

"Elizabeth, what are you doing home?"

"I'm not home anymore. I'm leaving."

John raced after her and jumped in the car just as she sped off. He insisted that she let him explain. She drove in a blind fury out of the city, toward the Great Swamp.

"I can't let you go like this."

"This is what you do when you're away from me?"

"I'm never away from you. I belong to you."

"Stop saying that!"

She drove on. "How many?" she hissed at him a moment later. "How many women, how many times?"

"Just Gloria. And only the one thing."

"Next you're going to tell me that all the time she was doing it to you, you were thinking of me."

He was surprised at the question. "Yes, I was," he said in that way of his, so open, so devoid of artifice. She half believed him.

And half didn't. "What is the big deal, John? What is the hang-up?"

"I only make love to you."

"But this other thing, this is what you dream about. Like in the magazines."

"...I can't stop thinking of it. Of you."

"Stop!!" my Elizabeth cried. She slid the car off the highway and into a muddy swamp trail. A few feet in, the thick foliage swallowed them completely, creepers and palms around them where the roof of the convertible would have been.

Elizabeth bolted from her door and walked around to his side. John was just getting out of his seat when she pushed him back down. Her face was set and grim as she yanked his knees from under the dashboard and turned them toward her. Then she knelt down in the soft earth in the doorway.

In a twinkling, his pants were undone and around his knees. His organ was enormous and ripe. His eyes could not decide if they wanted to watch or not. His whole frame trembled with the anticipation as she brought her lips slowly closer. He felt her breath exhale onto him.

"Elizabeth," he said in delirium.

"You shut up. Save your breath for croaking at the moon."

She ran a moistening tongue once over her lips and then brought them down decisively, the whole length of him in a single motion. John came at once. And toggled. The Big Note wafted through the swampland, where it seemed very much at home.

"You can just stay that way for a while," she muttered as she stood up. "At least until I can trust you out of my sight."

Oh, the bitter irony of those words. How often, in the nights that followed, would I hear my Elizabeth crying herself to sleep and know that the echo of this epithet was the cause.

We can only surmise what happened next, but it is logical. My Elizabeth's indignation did not disappear right away. She tossed you into the back seat, and backed the car onto the highway. On the way back to the city, she stopped to buy gasoline. I know the place, by the Bayou Petitjohn. She went inside a minute. There are trees overhead, and snakes, and the car roof was collapsed. A snake lands behind you on top of the trunk. There is only one escape–to the muddy ground. The snake follows. Your mind cannot think now, only react. You see the safety of the Bayou and make for it. You leap in...and the waters of the Great Swamp close over your head for the next five years.

Those years were mine.

I came recommended. If one wanted to find big frog in the Great Swamp, one came to me, Jean-Paul Olivier. I was the top man, the dog with the nose. Many thousands of them I had sent to the tables of New Orleans, fresh from the end of my three-pronged spear. No skiff drifted more silently than mine through sultry backwaters on a dense summer's night. No one had my eyes for their eyes, that sudden iridescence in the flashlight beam. No wrist gave the gig a swifter snap, no aim was more accurate.

I do not boast. I had no need to boast with her. I had come recommended.

She stood on the stairs of my little house on the Bayou Anglais, her gray eyes still red in the fringes from days of weeping. I loved her at once.

"Of course, Miss, I can get frog for you. How many pound?"

"No, no," she said, horrified. "A certain frog."

"Ah, a trophy."

"No, no, alive. He must be alive."

"But I am a frog killer, Miss."

"I don't know where else to go," she said and began to weep silently.

I invited her in. She told me she was a scientist searching for a particular kind of bullfrog, for an experiment. I did not believe that but I could refuse her nothing.

That night and for long weeks to come we drifted along the bank of the Bayou Petitjohn near where she had last seen you. Each night we widened the search. At first she insisted on compensating me, for she would not permit me to gig those who were not you. I took her money, out of courtesy, and I took down the prize skins from my trophy wall, for I could see they disturbed her. We searched and searched, but you were nowhere to be found.

I did not wish to deepen her sorrow, but after a time, I felt she should know the odds. So one night I took her to the center of the Great Swamp–at least the center as I know it. I threw my arms to all points of the compass and told her: eighty miles this and eighty miles that, all swamp. She understood at once and hung her head. It was then I told her that the odds meant nothing to me. That I would continue searching as along as she would stay. That I would devote my life to her. That I loved her. She wept.

I can chart our years together in many ways. One way is to look at the map of the swamps she kept nailed to the door of our little bedroom. Over the first years, in green squares, she recorded our quest for you. Later, we went over the same water again, and she blocked it in red. Black was the last color she used, until the map was a solid blot and her hope of finding you obliterated with it.

Slowly she came to trust me. I never pressed her, the way I might have with Marie Calvert or one of the D'Urville cousins. We spent more and more time together. She began to stay in my house over the weekends rather than return to her house by the university. I moved out my taxidermy equipment and made her a place in my spare room. Soon she was spending a week at a time, sleeping days, searching nights.

My Elizabeth trusted me with her body first and only much later with her secret. I have known both kinds of women. Some will tell you all they know, reveal every last scrap of identity before parting their knees even a little inch. Others are more seductive–they know that the intimacies of the soul are the prize and those of the body are only the wrapping.

I accepted her body without reservation, that first time on the pine needles of the Isle Duquesne and all the many times thereafter. But I confess, I could not believe her secret. "I have to tell you the truth, Jean-Paul," she said, when we had known each other a year. "Even if it drives you away."

"Nothing could ever..." I started to say.

She held her fingers to my lips and told me. Soon afterward, she gave me her journal to read. What was I to think? That she was insane? That she was dangerous? That I could not, after hearing her fantastic story, ever believe anything she would say again? No. I believed what her eyes and her arms told me. And if she was crazy, mon *ami*, what a tender craziness it was. To spend her life searching for someone she had loved and lost? To weigh safe anchor with only two lips for a compass? To peel back the rigid shell of rights and measured equalities and go soft into the world? One must love such a crazy woman.

There is one more way I chart our years together. She came to me because I had been recommended, Jean-Paul Olivier, frog hunter. I had never seen the Great Swamp as anything but a livelihood. Over the years, my Elizabeth taught me to see the beauty of it. And the reason of it, the simple, natural order beneath the chaos. Soon after she arrived, I killed my last *grenouille*.

Still, when I saw you, my first thought was to throw. Even after five years, I continued to travel with my old three-pronged frog gig, against snakes and the like. A quick flick of the wrist and you would be just another easy meal for the gator. She would be free of you and so would I.

But I did not kill you, John Surrey. You seemed eager for the net and your markings were precisely the way my Elizabeth had described them. I brought you aboard the skiff. Better to take you back, I thought. Once she has found you and kissed you and nothing happens, she will overcome her delusion and I will have her.

She knew something had happened the moment my skiff touched the pier. She stood in the door to the little house and watched as I walked up from the bayou, the canvas sack heavy in my hand. "A turtle?" she asked.

"My love," I whispered, "I have found him."

My answer staggered her. A hand went to her forehead and she looked pale. "John," she said, struggling for breath.

She approached the kitchen table where I had placed the bag and slowly untied the cord. What I saw next cannot be denied. As you vaulted from the bag and into her arms, a small cry of pure joy leapt from her throat. Then she crushed you to her lips. The windows of my little house were suddenly in fragments. The tin roof groaned against the rafters, as if a giant hand wanted to twist it off. The Big Note was not meant to be played indoors, you see. It was a hundred times louder than the fog horn at Pont Timbalier but also sweet and full of melody, as the horn is not.

Ten years in the Great Swamp had strengthened my Elizabeth. Where she had held you a moment ago, she now held a fully grown young man, Mr. John Surrey, completely off the floor and hugged him with all her might.

"Elizabeth," he croaked, "I'm so sorry...."

That night, I stayed away from the little house. My exile was on the bayou, on the end of the dock, with a bottle of Kentucky bourbon in my hand. I could not bear to see them together.

About midnight, my Elizabeth came and joined me. "He's asleep," she said. "He will sleep a lot, these first days."

"It was the truth," I said. "All these years."

"All these years you didn't believe me."

"To tell the truth—no."

"But you loved me anyway." She gave me a very sweet kiss, as full of love as I can remember.

I asked the terrible question. "What will you do now?"

She did not answer; she had something else on her mind. "He's very young, isn't he? Or rather, I'm five years older. He noticed, he touched me here." She stroked the merest of age lines in her beautiful forehead.

"He must have been very young when you met."

"No," my Elizabeth said, "he was the same age. I don't think he gets older, Jean-Paul, at least not when he's...the other way."

"Frog."

"Yes."

"But if he never gets older..."

"Then he would live forever...if he stayed the other way."

We were silent for a moment as the bayou waters trickled under the dock. "He seems very devoted to you," I observed.

"He says he belongs to me. He has always said that. But it isn't so. No one belongs to anyone else. No one has the right to stand in the way of someone's destiny. Their potential."

"Potential?" I laughed. "To sit in the mud and eat flies?"

"To live a dozen lives, in a dozen centuries."

"But you said he doesn't remember."

"Does that matter? You paint the skiff once a year. Do you remember what color it was six years ago?"

"No."

"But you're still proud of the way it looks every spring. And proud of the way it floats" –her voice became distant– "to all new, wonderful places."

"You want set him floating again?"

My Elizabeth did not answer.

"I thought you loved him."

She answered: "I wonder if I love him enough."

She kissed me again and then went back to him. I nursed the bottle for some hours more. Once, twice, inside the house, she cried. Then, about dawn, I heard a faint harmony on the mist.

So, now I have completed the task I promised her I would do. You are over the side and kicking like mad for the green bottom. I know I will never see you again–today, my friend, we are both a little lost in the Great Swamp.

And I will be lost when I return home, too. Because I know what I will find: an empty bed, a long note, and my Elizabeth gone.

The note will be painful to read. She will say she still loves me and I will believe her. I will believe, too, that she could never stay here in the Great Swamp, not after what she has done. Every night she would hear their chorus of voices and die inside. Rather, she will go on, my beautiful Elizabeth, and enrich the world. It gave her a miracle and she gave it back.

I will never leave. They say we Cajun dry up like old pepper pods if we leave the water. And it will not be so painful for me. Once I heard their song in the thick night air and thought only of slaughter and the scales of the marketplace. Now I will hear them and I will remember love, and that part of love which is magic.

In my little house on the Bayou Anglais I will have such memories every night. There, perhaps, is your happily ever after.

JUST TOUCH IT

Jim Boroughs was not a serious *aficionado* of crackpot theories. He didn't much care, at least anymore, who shot Kennedy or whether Ike had made a lopsided deal with the gray aliens. He did still enjoy a bit of homespun illogic to get one through the day, however. He embraced the knowledge that a lit cigarette will call the bus or that identical twins are always fucking with you and are, therefore, never to be trusted.

"What exactly is the timing of this?" Peter asked him.

"I don't know. Midnight to midnight, I guess."

Peter Brooks was Jim's best friend and had always enjoyed his friend's quirky ideas and schemes. He was so curious about the current one that he had agreed to arrange the experiment. He had laid in the food, fuel, beer and smoke. He had conspired with the charter company to fast-shuffle a few reservations and secured their favorite sloop, *Circe.*

"So, if you don't set foot on land for twenty-four hours over your birthday, your fortieth birthday, then you won't get any older. Time won't count. Like Ezekiel stopping the sun."

"That was Joshua."

"How did you cook up this theory?"

"I was swimming off Zuma last summer and it just came to me: kill gravity, kill age. I mean, age isn't anything except how big a hold gravity's got on you. Pulls you down, yanks your gut out over your belt, bends the backs of old men. Look where you go when it finally wins–right into the ground with it. But out there, in the big blue water..."

Peter smiled and shook his three-years-younger head in admiration. "How can you be so old and so weird?"

"You too shall reach the Twisted Time," Jim replied in his *Tales from the Crypt* voice. "You are not yet forty, my son."

"Neither are you, yet."

"But like pilots say, the scary thing is the approach, not the touchdown."

"And you aren't planning on touching down."

"Correct."

> *Farewell to thee, dear Kingston girls,*
> *Farewell to St. Andrew's Dock,*
> *If ever we should come back again,*
> *We'll make your cradles rock....*

Gregor Konstantine spotlighted his entrance with song, in this case an old sea shanty sung at bravura volume. Peter was one of the few people who found this habit amusing. With just-pumped muscles under an obviously oiled skin, Gregor was wearing nothing but spandex bikini briefs and a heat-seeking smile. He was one of Peter's performer friends, valued on these jaunts because he rarely got seasick and actually knew how to sail.

"Hello, men." Gregor piped himself aboard with a theatrical lisp. "Off to sea in a manful manner?"

The resident boat owners on the dock gaped at Gregor and then cast scathing looks down at Peter, as if to say, we tolerate you weekend skippers because you usually take your worst habits (and friends) with you out to sea. Peter looked back, as if to say, we're going, we're gone.

The diesel turned over with a whump. "Jim, bow lines, please."

They could have sailed the first leg, but that was uphill today, in light winds, and Jim was eager to escape the shadow of gravity. For the next hour, as the diesel rumbled under the cockpit floor, they drank afternoon Heinekens and talked about the party.

It was the best party they had been to in a long time, all agreed, including Gregor, who had crashed hundreds. Jim's wife, Caroline, had festooned their garage in sixties posters and lighting (blacks and strobes). And she had made the 20-something disc jockey earn his fee. She had gone over his play list, found it lousy with featherweight techno/disco, and sent the kid cruising the record shops for a week, playing the unsatisfied customer until he'd bagged some real and enduring tunes.

The kid started spinning at nine and didn't stop until the polite insistence of the LAPD officer at four. Everyone danced. No one could stop dancing. People who had benched themselves for fifteen years jacked straight up when they heard that rock and roll tom-tom. They couldn't resist it; there was no one left to tie them to the mast. The music, the beer, the drugs, the dense incense. It had been a transforming experience.

"It was the Motown that got me. That fucking beat, how can you resist it?"

"You can't."

"Great fucking party."

"And you guys remember all those lyrics," Gregor remarked.

"The memory is powerful, my son," Jim responded. "You'll know, when you get old enough to have one."

Gregor smiled endurance. "Okay. That's all right. I'm ready for all the 'kid' jokes. I figured that would be the price of this trip. I'm willing to pay to get out of the smog and away from the phone for a few days."

"Lots of auditions, Greeg?" Peter asked.

"No auditions. I'm cold. When I say the phone, I mean the phone at work."

"You're not back in the boiler room."

"I am, yes." This topic soured Gregor's mood. He stood up and went forward, peeling off the spandex bikini and sprawling himself naked on the foredeck in the warming sun.

Jim relieved Peter at the helm. Inside the diesel's bubble of sound, they could talk privately. "That's a shame. He hates that fucking boiler room. I'd hate it, too–making cold calls all day, pissed-off people just flat hanging up on you."

"That's what I do–hang up. So do you, I've seen you."

"I feel sorry for him. He's not a bad actor, you know."

"I know, you took me to his play. I just…"

"What?"

"I can't feel too sorry for Gregor Konstantine."

"No?"

"Christ, for one thing he's thirty-three. He won't be in that boiler room forever. He's free to leave. He can start out in something new and not worry about the kids' college fund. Or he's free to stay. He could decide that acting's not his thing after all. He could decide that, or something else, or anything."

"You envy that."

"Don't you? Hell, I remember when everything I owned could be carried on my back."

"Sounds like the first line of a country song."

Jim stood up behind the wheel. "Pretty pathetic," he said without irony, "when your fondest memories become clichés."

"I didn't mean..."

"You ready to open up a little?"

Peter hesitated, then realized Jim was referring to their course. They had passed the R-10 buoy and could now open their angle to wind and sail the rest of the way to Catalina, their destination. "Right," he agreed, and reached down to choke the fuel from the diesel.

"What?" Gregor cried lazily from the bow.

"We're going to sail."

"In a minute," Jim said, and in the next breath scissored his legs over the lifeline and plunged butt first into the sea.

"Jim!" Peter shouted in startled reflex. His friend's head grew smaller as the boat's momentum carried it away. But Jim waved. "Fight gravity!" he shouted.

Gregor scampered astern. "All right!" he cried and made for the gunwale. But Peter grabbed his wrist.

"No."

"I just want to cool off, man."

"Let him be by himself."

"He doesn't own the fucking ocean."

"Today, he does."

The sight of Catalina looming larger by the minute had a predictable effect on Gregor Konstantine–he felt the urge to party. While they were still thirty minutes out, he brought a vial of pills out on deck. "Organic mescaline, the best. All the punch with none of the lunch, if you get what I mean. It's a real body trip, this stuff–makes you feel you're made out of butter."

"I got arteries like that."

"Not for me," Peter said. "Somebody's got to get us to a mooring. But go ahead, Jim."

"No, I don't think so."

"Come on. Shake you outta those birthday blues."

"No," Jim said and went below.

Gregor looked at Peter for some kind of explanation but Peter just shrugged. Gregor knocked back a capsule with a hit of beer. "Okay, see you over the rainbow, tin man."

Jim stayed below until a pair of cries roused him from his slumber on the settee berth. The first was a wail from Gregor, something like "Ahhhh-yah," clear evidence that the mushrooms were kicking in. But then Peter also shouted. "Jim, we've got an escort!"

A pod of pilot whales darted along *Circe's* port side as they headed into the shallow harbor. The black tubes of muscle and blubber moved with no discernible effort just ahead of the bow. In the early days of sailing ships, Jim had read, the appearance of whales at landfall was a good omen. It meant the arriving ship would be welcomed and that business ashore would be profitable. He, of course, had no business ashore.

It was about this time that Gregor spotted the first of the girls. The harbor was pretty full for a Monday evening in early summer. A number of power boats swung at the big moorings furthest offshore and there were several lithe female figures reclining on the decks of these motorized behemoths.

"Hello, girls!" Gregor cried at the top of his lungs. "Pete! Pete, steer for this one over here."

"We're going for a mooring, Greg. Get a hold on."

"Get some clothes on," Jim added.

"I am come out of the sea!" Gregor bellowed. "A Greek God to delight mortal woman."

They dropped sails and inched closer on the engine. Gregor was howling. Heads on the moored craft began to turn. They passed close to the most outlying boat, a fifty-foot cruiser named *Penultimate*. A young girl on the flying bridge watched Gregor's passing with wide eyes.

Farewell to thee, dear Kingston girls,
Farewell to St. Andrew's Dock...

"Get your fucking pants on!" a skipper shouted.

If ever we should come back again,
We'll bring our lovely cocks....

"Get your lovelies inside that swimsuit!" Jim insisted.

Gregor complied, sliding his torso into the elastic, day-glo modesty strip. It only enhanced his mushroom-driven lasciviousness. His eyes roved the harbor, moving rhythmically from the mature beauties coming up portside, down to his own imprisoned stem, back to the women.

"Do you *see* it?!" he asked them at broadcast volume.

They looked puzzled.

"Just *touch* it!" he pleaded.

Now they understood. Some giggled.

"Just touch it!" Gregor continued to bleat. They passed another boat with teenaged girls on the fantail, also giggling. An older man, a dad, hustled onto the deck, gesticulating angrily. "You can touch it, too!" Gregor offered.

The sloop crept up on a mooring wand. "How about this?" Peter asked, trying to ignore the activity on the foredeck.

"It's right in the middle of the harbor."

"You think we should anchor in a more isolated spot?"

He cast a look forward, toward their Poseidon. "Or break out the leg irons."

"You got a point." Peter put the helm over and headed *Circe* toward Cherry Cove, a smaller shelter just north of the main anchorage. It was mostly empty.

"Hey! Where are we going? The girls are over here!"

They ignored him.

"Just touch it!" he moaned in parting.

Sunset was at 6:45 that evening. By that time, Gregor Konstantine had already been gone for two hours. They had helped him inflate the Zodiac and launched him toward the main harbor, willing to risk charges of criminal complicity just to get rid of him. "I'm going nuts on this boat," he kept muttering, eyes spinning in counter-convections. "There's no place to walk."

Now Peter was beginning to feel cabin fever, too. When he spotted the shore boat nearby he ran a small pennant to the spreaders, the signal for a pickup.

"I'm staying," said Jim.

"Why? The no-touchee-land thing doesn't start until midnight, right? A man should have a few drinks in the last hours of his youth."

"I've got drinks here. I've got everything I'll need."

The shore boat was approaching and Peter was torn. "I can stay, Jim…"

"Go."

"But I think I should go round him up, you know. Who knows what he's got his nose into."

"Five'll get you ten, it smells like fish."

Peter grinned. "Probably right." The shore boat came alongside. "You sure you're okay?"

"Go."

"I'll be back soon."

Jim made himself some canned spaghetti and ate it on deck along with a stiff glass of Stoly. A half hour later the band started up in the club ashore, rock and roll classics kicked off with a Best of Beatles medley. The music crept across the still waters of the cove toward him but it failed to get his spirits pumping the way it had the night of his party. The old tunes seemed mournful now, tinny, small.

Later, as he sat there in the full darkness, back against the cabin bulkhead, Jim Boroughs got the feeling that he was being watched. Never had he felt this sensation more distinctly. He stood up slowly and looked toward the main harbor and the three dozen craft at mooring. Most all of them were dark, shut down for the night or abandoned for the bright lights of shore. He pulled the binoculars from the companionway shelf and scanned the harbor. He could find no one looking back.

So he put the glasses away and stretched out again. What the hell, let them look, he thought. He cupped his groin. "Just touch it," he whispered.

Jim was awakened by a pounding on *Circe's* hull. Someone at sea level outside was trying to make himself heard.

"Hey, in there, wake up!"

Jim rolled over and looked down the length of the cabin to discover Peter asleep across the settee berth. There was no sign of Gregor.

"Hey, aboard?"

Jim swung his feet carefully to the floor and stumbled through his vodka hangover to the companionway and the deck. A guy in his sixties bobbed alongside in a skiff.

"You skipper?"

"I guess."

"You got a friend, black hair, rowing an Avon-4?"

"Yeah. Where is he?"

"Stepped on an urchin, got him a couple spines in the ankle. Looks real bad. They sent me to get you."

Peter was sleeping off his poison, in this case rum, and it took several minutes to get him completely awake. Pretty soon they were all three in the skiff, squinting across the harbor under an already hateful sun. Jim noticed that the swell was unusually deep and long. High overhead, long cirrus clouds streaked the length of the sky. "Something moving in?" Jim asked the old guy rowing.

"Ain't heard the NOA this morning. But I'll betcha."

"Did you see Greeg last night?" Jim asked Peter.

"No. He never came into the bar."

"How was it?"

"Like always–you know."

"That's why I didn't go."

They didn't say much more–it hurt to talk. But ten minutes later, when the guy in the skiff deposited Jim and Peter at the swim platform of a forty-five-foot Grand Banks and they climbed up to discover Gregor, their own small agonies faded away. He was lying on a deck chair covered in a blanket, still wearing the same bikini swimsuit. His complexion was battleship gray and his skin was hot and dry to the touch. He was just barely conscious, delirious.

"Greeg, what happened to you?"

"I....I just need a moment of your time, sir, to acquaint you with our offer."

"Take all the time you want, buddy."

"Please don't hang up, sir."

"I won't hang up."

Jim looked around at the others on the spacious teak afterdeck. There were several college girls, gorgeous and wide-eyed in their sleepwear bikinis, and a few slightly older men. Aggressive types. NASDAQ millionaires. They told him what had happened. Gregor had rowed over to them late the preceding afternoon. (Still roaring on the 'shrooms, Jim calculated.) He had called out to the girls to go swimming. A couple of them had complied (they being mortals and Gregor a Greek God come out of the sea). He had complained that he had a pain in his leg but soon after that they started drinking strawberry margaritas (what else?) and he never said another thing. They hadn't seen him pass out on the lounger last night (likely story) and this was the condition in which they had discovered him this morning. The boat's owner wanted it understood that he was not liable. His buddy backed him up and he was "a prominent attorney." Jim replied that he was not "a prominent attorney" but that he could easily procure one, giving the verb lots of pimp twist.

"Hey, aboard." It was the old man in the skiff again, with an athletic-looking man in his late forties as passenger. "I brought a doctor."

Dr. Mike Gardner introduced himself. He was moored nearby on his *Penultimate* and had heard the old man's pleas as he had canvassed the anchorage. He examined Gregor, whose left foot was double its normal size and nearly black. "Been leaping without looking?" he asked the actor. He probed the puffiest area.

"Don't touch it!" screamed Greeg.

"Sorry...Bad luck: the spines have gone right to a vein. Maybe if we had seen this last night, I could have removed them. But too much toxin has been released."

Peter was shocked. "He's not going to die?"

"He might, without treatment. We have to get anti-toxin started and transport him to the mainland for surgery." The doctor stood up and looked out over the harbor. "There is a helicopter service out of Avalon. I'll see if I can arrange it." He turned to the boat's owner. "Can I use your radio?"

Dr. Mike disappeared below. Jim and Peter looked at each other. "What a bad break," Peter muttered. "I'm sorry about the trip, man."

"Jesus, that's not important. Let's concentrate on saving the fucking guy's life."

"Pete..." Gregor whispered.

They bent down next to the lounger. The heat from Gregor's fever convected in the air around him. "Right here, Greeg."

"Don't leave me alone. Promise, Pete."

"I'll stay with you."

"Damn!" came a cry from below. The doctor stormed up on deck. "The pilot won't take him without a licensed health care professional aboard. Got an insurance problem, he says. As if I don't know about that." He looked around the deck. "I don't suppose any of you qualifies?"

"I arrange venture capital for..."

"I'm a senior partner with..."

"We cut film," Peter and Jim announced

"Worthless!" the doctor bellowed. "Now I'm going to have to go!"

"Worthless," he said again.

So, Jim spent his birthday alone, swinging at mooring beyond the reach of age and gravity. He'd gotten his wish. Now he'd just sit here until Peter returned, like he'd sat there the night before, or in his hotel room in New York, in New Orleans, in London, purposely not going to the clubs, the pubs, purposely not going ashore to hear the band. Sit there, alone, unable to deceive himself, knowing the reason why.

He took another long swig of beer. "Worthless," the doctor had muttered. Jim knew he was not worthless; that was not the demon that haunted him. He could thank the Fates for that. A lot of his colleagues, particularly that group of cutters at the studio who were a little older than he, they'd had the worth problem. In the coffee room, or many times at Ernie's Taco House after work, the tequilas would wash down and they would ask (sometimes out loud): What had their working lives added up to? Günter Grunthaler had cut nearly every episode of the studio's only certified hit series and was considered a real corporate asset, but it was still an action/cop/crash thing, nothing like the fine personal films he had done in Germany as a young man. Davey Quarles had nearly drunk himself to death, the rude, quarrelsome bastard. Jim knew a half dozen such guys who were on final approach to fifty, profoundly divorced or never married, who cobbled together mass-market car chases without any greater ambition, and who, on weekends, gambled or flew or fished with a certain desperate proficiency. He sympathized with them, but he was not like them.

"Worthless" was not the problem. Invisible was the problem.

There was a tug at the line Jim had rigged over the transom. The rod bent partway down, then snapped back. Jim got up and reeled in the double-hook rig. No need to hurry. True to form, the savvy harbor fish had deftly consumed the bait without committing themselves to the hook. Jim tore off another couple of hunks of Velveeta cheese, re-baited and watched it all sink to the bottom. He could see them down there, Garibaldi, a foot long, sheep-headed reef fish as bright gold as a cheap necklace whose preferred food is a processed cheese product. L.A.'s corner of the Pacific supported a food-chain worthy of a Disney opium nightmare.

A blast of cold air raked the cove and Jim shivered. Out in the more exposed part of the harbor, he could see that the swell had increased since morning. The Grand Banks, from which Gregor had been evacuated around noon, along with Peter and the doctor, was now evacuating itself. The two money-managers could be seen on the foredeck horsing the mooring loop free of the Sampson post. A number of boats had opted to leave.

Jim tuned in the weather as he got himself another beer and heard NOA predicting that a strong squall line would sweep the islands later that night. It was unusual weather for that time of year. For a moment he put on his skipper's hat: *Circe* was in a well-sheltered position with massive ground tackle. This curve of rocky shore was his friend and protector, so long as he didn't set foot on it that day.

His wrist watch alarm sounded softly. It was 4:19. He had promised Peter he would monitor channel 24 at twenty minutes after every hour. He hadn't heard anything from Peter all afternoon, but when he tuned in the VHF at 4:20, his buddy's voice could be heard through a maze of static, already broadcasting. "...calling the vessel *Circe*, I say again, do you copy, over?"

"This is *Circe*, good to hear you, Pete. How's Gregor doing? Over."

"He's doing okay. Chopper ride was hairy, he convulsed a few times..."

"Jesus..."

"The chopper pilot can't bring us back tonight. There's a front moving through. Over."

"I know, it's already beginning to pipe up. I'm glad we went for the cove, over."

"Right. So, listen, the doctor that helped Greeg is here, he wants to ask a favor, I'm putting him on." The doctor's voice sounded tired. "Mr. Boroughs, my boat is the *Penultimate*, in the center of the harbor, do you see her? Over."

"Looking at her. Seems to be riding okay. Over."

"That mooring should hold. I own it–it's six tons of concrete. But I'm worried about the lines if it really blows up tonight. My wife's no sailor..."

"Most everybody's cleared out of the cove. I could move her in closer now. Over."

There was no immediate answer. Jim smiled, savoring a bit of long distance schadenfreude at the doctor's expense. His $400,000 boat, in the hands of a "worthless" somebody he doesn't even know? Now he'd be asking Pete. Pete would be saying, yeah, Jim, sure, he can handle it. "Uh, okay, thanks, why don't you do that. Over."

"Sure will. Anything else? Over."

Pete came back on. "Keep your feet off the beach. I'm still watching the results of this experiment. I'll call back at 0900 tomorrow. So long."

"This is the San Pedro Marine Operator, clear with the *Circe*."

Jim planned to take a quick peek through *Circe's* onboard Chapman's to review the techniques of driving big power boats but there was a strong blast of wind just then and he decided that it would be best not to wait. If the wind got any higher, the normally easy dinghy row to the *Penultimate* might end up on a Baja beach.

Two minutes later he was in the inflatable raft, pulling toward the cruiser. Everything was fine inside the cove, but once the dinghy hit the weather outside the point, the ride came to resemble his son's favorite attraction at Disneyland–the Mad Hatter's Teacups. The French-made plastic oars proved useless as bow became stern, and then switched again in the rising wind. "God damn it!" As hard as he strained at the oars, his vector toward *Penultimate* widened until he was rowing into the wind just to stay even.

And he realized now that *Penultimate* had much higher decks than a sailing boat–would there be anything to hold onto once, if, he got there? Beyond the doctor's boat was the bell buoy and beyond that the channel. His earlier musing about Mexican beaches was rapidly becoming less and less humorous.

Penultimate loomed up large, partly obscured in the flying spray. Jim worked at the oars as hard and fast as he could, his heart digging for salvation but his mind's over-the-shoulder trigonometry dashing the hope–he would not be quite able to reach the boat's stern counter. This was really fucked. Suddenly, a length of line spun out from the deck of the cruiser. Somebody was aboard and it was somebody with a pretty good arm, too. The line landed in the hissing sea just a few feet from him. In a second he had snagged the line and secured it to the raft. In less than a minute, he stood on the deck of *Penultimate,* drenched, winded, arms leaden, thanking his rescuer.

"I didn't rescue you."

"I was on my way to Ensenada."

"Isn't that a long way, in a little boat like that?"

Jim laughed. "No, no, I mean, if you hadn't thrown that line...Anyway, I got here okay. Doctor Gardner called me on the radio. He's...your father, I guess?"

"Dad called you?"

"It was my friend he took on the helicopter. I told him I'd move his boat into the cove. Ahead of the storm. I'm Jim Boroughs."

"Susan."

"Where's your mother?"

"On the island. With her camera."

"You didn't go?"

"I just didn't feel like going. Not this trip."

Jim was silent for a moment. "Well, I'm glad you were here," he said finally.

"To rescue you."

"Yes."

Susan Gardner was sixteen, maybe an early seventeen. Quite a pretty girl, with short brown hair and green eyes. Jim noticed at once, too, that she was very confident. There was no girlishness in Susan, no retreat to any coy, manufactured incompetence.

Jim saw this immediately, for their first obligation was to get *Penultimate* into shelter. A quick look at the nearly chafed ground tackle made Jim glad he had suggested moving the boat. "Another hour and this would have worn right through,"

"Then I would have been off for Mexico."

"Right. But you could have started the engines and come back."

"Maybe I would. Maybe I'd just keep going."

He showed her how to free the mooring line once he powered the cruiser up into the wind a bit; then later, when they got up into the cove, how to reverse the procedure and snag the new mooring wand and loop.

Susan listened carefully and got it the first time. From his perch on the flying bridge, he could watch her working on the foredeck. He nudged *Penultimate* into position and she laced the heavy lines on and off the capstan drum with evident strength. Really, he could *see* her strength, through a thin athletic bra that flexed over a tightly muscled back. In fact, Jim permitted his eyes to follow her all over the deck. It had been a very long time since he had taken such a lingering and detailed look at a young girl.

She looked up at him. "Okay? Did I do it right?"

"Looks fine. I'm coming down." He killed the engines and clambered down the narrow chrome ladder to the deck. "It really makes a difference, doesn't it?"

"What?"

"Being in the cove. Out of the wind. Sheltered."

"Is that your boat?"

"Yeah." *Circe* was just a few moorings over, the only other boat in the cove. "I put us close together, in case, you know, in case we need each other. Tonight."

"Is it going to be that bad?"

"We'll be fine, just the two of us."

Susan gave Jim a cock of her head. "There's my mother, too."

"I meant, just the two boats."

They sat in silence for a few minutes, watching the cliffs above them. It was actually sort of pretty, now that the danger was behind them. The wind had begun to rage in earnest and the cliff tops were streaming white banners of cloud, scud lashing through with the force of the whole Pacific. The water outside in the channel went dark gray, then a low, silvery black, still too blasted by the descending air mass to get up and dance. That would come later in the night, the big seas, the rogue waves. Inside the cove the surface was glassy and dull, the crystal water grown opaque, the golden Garibaldi fish muted to dull brass.

Jim broke the silence. "Was there a reason you didn't go with your mother? I mean, it must be pretty boring for you, stuck on the boat all day."

"I wanted boring. I'm sick of people."

"What people? All people?"

"Most people. They sent me to this new school. I liked the school I was at, but, no, it wasn't 'preparing' me. And these kids are so...into themselves. You see them in the hall and they look right through you, like you're not even there. But I am there, you know." She stopped, feeling Jim's eyes on her, intent and reflective. She returned his gaze. "I suppose that sounds really stupid to you."

"You'd be surprised how not stupid that sounds to me."

From the enclosed bridge of the cruiser there came a rasp of static, a tinny voice. "Is that your VHF?" They went aft and into the well-appointed main cabin. The radio was next to the steering station and a female voice was rasping through the air. Susan rolled her eyes.

"...Susan, what's wrong, can't you answer me? Susan, where are you? Where's the boat, why did you move the boat?"

Susan picked up the mike. "I'm okay, Mom. We moved the boat to get out of the wind. Dad asked a guy to help us."

"What guy?"

Susan handed the mike to Jim with an expression that read: You speak the language. "This is Jim Boroughs, Mrs. Gardner. It was my friend your husband took to the mainland. Just tell the shore boat we're in Cherry Cove. Over."

"The shore boat isn't running, they say it's too rough. You'll have to come in and get me. I'm on the dock...."

"If it's too rough for the shore boat, I don't know how I'm going to land. Over."

But it was clear she had talked over his transmission. "...On the dock by the gas pumps." The connection dissolved into static.

"Mom," Susan tried with an exasperated tone but there was no answer. They went out on deck. It was rougher than before. "It's ridiculous," Susan declared. "You don't have to do it. There's a hotel."

"Well, Susan, I can try, at least." The girl looked pale and worried, now. Jim hesitated, then reached out and drew her under his shoulder into a swift, one-armed embrace. She laced an arm around his waist for a quick moment. "But you stand by with that throwing line again, okay?"

"Okay."

Within the hour, he was back aboard *Penultimate,* naked under a scalding shower, sipping a thick tumbler of scotch while a hint of codeine-flavored Tylenol slowly infused his bloodstream with warmth from the inside out.

The cruiser carried a hard-chined dinghy on stern davits powered by a five-horse outboard. Susan had helped him launch it, in favor of the Avon, and he had arrived off the end of the dock about ten minutes later. The seas were leaping wildly onto the shallow beach from which the dock jutted. There was no way on earth the dinghy could approach the fuel dock, let alone take a passenger off. Even Mrs. Gardner must have realized this, because she had abandoned the spray-blasted gas pumps and stood now on the beach, in a kind of pose, as if she were hailing a cross-town bus. She had a huge boxy object with her, on a tripod.

"Yes, I see you," Jim had muttered to himself. "What am I supposed to do now?"

"Come in!" she cried.

"Can't!" Jim responded. "Too rough!"

He had cast his eye along the crescent of the beach and spotted a large rocky outcropping near one end. Abutting the cliffs, it formed a small shelter from the waves. He pointed the dink in that direction to take a closer look. Onshore, Mrs. Gardner looked perturbed to have had to move from the dock, but she slung the camera–that's what it was, a huge old-style box camera–over her shoulder and followed Jim's lead.

The lee created by the rocks was small and subject to surge. But by the time Mrs. Gardner had schlepped her Ansel Adams to the spot, Jim had worked the dink into the lee and found a small piece of beach where a very wet landing might be attempted. It was a little easier to communicate out of the direct wind.

"I can try it here. Get ready."

He took the outboard out of gear, kicked it up out of the water, and rowed the bow around to face the sea, slowly backing the dingy into the beach. It was tricky work and he had gotten totally soaked by slap-happy waves bouncing off the cliffs. He moved into about three feet of water, wading depth, but the lady hadn't moved off the beach.

"You have to come out to me," Jim bellowed.

"No, I can't. My gear will get wet."

"It's going to get wet anyway. Come on! It's only a few feet deep!"

He held his position and she held hers. "My husband brings the boat right up on shore."

"Not in this, he wouldn't."

"Can't you jump out and pull it up on the sand?"

Jump out and pull it up on the sand. It might have been possible. It wasn't that rough. Come away with just a few scrapes and bruises. Nothing broken, except a promise, and that was only one he'd made to himself. A silly promise, in service of an admittedly crackpot idea. How much could it matter?

He looked at his bare feet and at the sand of the beach. "No," he said.

"What do you mean?"

"I won't do it."

He kicked the outboard down into gear and spun out of the rocky shelter. Even with the solid mass of wind and spray in his face, he could hear the curses from the woman abandoned on the beach.

Later, as he stripped off his sea-drenched clothing in the doctor's cabin prior to jumping in the shower, he had heard the curses in greater detail, through the thin door. "He deliberately left me here, Susan. He could have come in and got me but he just left."

"He said it was too rough, Mom."

"Is he on the boat with you now?"

"He's taking a shower..."

"What?"

"He was freezing, from trying to get you, Mom. He doesn't have a shower on his sailboat."

"You tell him to go back to his own boat right this minute. Do you hear me? Do you hear?"

"Yes, Mom..."

He had found the Gardners' toiletries spread out on the head vanity, mostly creams and gels but layered with prescription bottles. The pain-killer was her mother's. Jim grinned as he popped one down his throat, looking forward to the languorous body glow he knew would follow. The perfect chemical companion for tonight: soothing the aches he knew his muscles were planning, then easing him off to sleep, wherever he ended up, with whatever other companion. So there–he had thought it out loud. The old man fantasizes in the shower. He even starts to get stiff. It was a sweet notion, even if pathetically wishful. Yet just when his rational, fully socialized voices begin to murmur him back to flaccidity, the door to the head had opened.

She had changed clothing. A skirt, a thin T-shirt, which clung to her in the steam. Jim's face peered through the cracked shower door. "Here," she said, and without modesty, like a lover of some weeks' boldness, and slipped a heavy glass tinkling with liquor and ice through the door into Jim's soapy hand. "It's some special stuff my dad likes."

"Thanks."

"I'm making us dinner."

Susan cooked him the big steak, the one her father had selected from Gelson's for his own dinner at anchor. It was too much meat for Jim but he ate it all anyway, plus more scotch and a couple of glasses of good Cabernet. Susan had a glass herself.

"If mom asks, I didn't have any."

"Your mother is never going to speak to me again."

"She'll forget. Dad'll forget. Anything that happens out here, they forget it all when they get back...into their whole thing."

Jim sat back in the plush settee. "That seems backwards to me."

"What do you mean?"

"You should remember this, and try to forget," he gestured toward shore, "that."

"What's that for you?"

"What?"

"Back on shore. What do you do?"

Jim sighed in reaction. The subject was bound to come up, it always did: So, what do you do for a living, old timer?

"I'm a film editor."

"Cool. I'm taking a film class this semester."

"Like it?"

"Yeah. My teacher said the editor is the one who saves the director's ass." Jim couldn't contain a laugh. "Whose ass have you saved, Jim?"

"Do you know Henry Graham?" he offered.

"The guy who does those sexy movies. With Mickey Rourke."

"I've worked for him. I wouldn't say I've exactly 'saved his ass,' though."

"Do you know Mickey Rourke?"

"I've met him."

"Did you do that film...uh, what was it...A Hundred Years Ago or something...."

"*One Hundred Years from Today?* Yeah, I cut that."

"How did they do that waterfall thing?"

And so it began: What had happened on this film? Who had done what? Was there really such a place? What's he really like? He couldn't fault Susan, she was just curious and show-biz was inherently interesting. It was just, damn it, here we go again: the rap, the block of good stories, the resume, not the man.

Jim Boroughs had a very good block of stories. From his years in theatre: the mishaps on live production, the broken legs at the top of Act Two, firemen crossing upstage with a hose, prop pigeons par-boiled by the heat of the lamps. From the movies: midnight exorcisms on a haunted location, overprotective boyfriends of ingénues going after directors with Bowie knives, hilarious cold readings in which big stars reveal their gaping ignorance, the obscene gestures, moonings and other exposures that wound up on the gag reel.

Jim did his duty; he told some of the better ones. Susan Gardener was enthralled, amused, horrified. At one point, she fell off the settee, gasping for breath between convulsions of laughter. When she climbed back up, it was onto Jim's side of the table, closer to him. He took her hand to make the next tale more intimate. She made no effort to draw it back. He hated it. This was fools' intimacy. The next well-told story would draw them farther apart. The next would set their course for the night–irreversibly toward clever, the reciprocal of need. This had happened so many times, his carpetbag of tricks proving more interesting than he himself. And there was a difference. There was.

He would not let it happen again. He made up an excuse. "Did you hear that?"

"What?"

"I don't know. I'm just going to check the mooring lines."

On deck, Jim saw that the sea had now closed him and Susan in completely. The world at the mouth of the cove was a hateful display of fury and blackness. *Circe* rode easily only yards away. There was a warmth slowly uncoiling in his legs and groin (the pain-killer) and a pleasant *in vino veritas* hypnosis in the way his eyes consumed the details of the night, of the storm, of Susan Gardner. Through the boat's windshield he watched her in the main cabin, fretting over minutiae, filling his wine glass again, sipping at her own, smoothing her skirt, running a comb through her hair. She seemed like a young girl trying to copy her mother's social graces. But her mother would have nothing to do with the decision Susan would make next. Jim dreaded going back inside, the way the Invisible Man must have dreaded sneaking into a crowded room. His secret would be lost if only one person could see him, and that one could see him naked.

"The boat's secure," he told Susan when he returned. "Maybe I should head home."

Susan's face fell. There was no mistaking her surprise and disappointment. "Why can't you stay here?"

"Well, I can. It's just..."

"I don't see any reason why you have to sit over there on your boat and I have sit here, alone."

Jim thought for a half second but could come up with no less adult way to say it. "Sitting's okay, Susan. The question is, where do we sleep?"

There was no confusion on Susan's face–she understood entirely. She clasped her knees to her breasts and smiled. "I'm not sleepy yet."

Jim smiled back. "Neither am I. But there's one thing."

"What?"

"I'm not going to tell any more stories. No more Hollywood gossip stuff, okay?"

"I liked that story."

"I'm glad but that was the last one, okay?"

"I'm not going to tell anybody."

"That's not it, Susan."

"Why?"

"I have my reasons, okay?"

"If you're going to act like my dad, you can go back to your boat."

That hurt. Jim collapsed of his own weight, his own age, into the settee and addressed himself to a huge glass of wine, drinking deeply.

Susan had a follow-through: "You're old enough to be my dad."

"No, I'm not."

"You're forty, at least."

"I'm not 'forty, at least.' I'm forty, exactly. Today." Susan raised her eyebrows. "'Happy Birthday' is what polite people say."

"Happy Birthday."

"And I am not old enough to be your dad. I met your dad. He *is* old enough to be your dad, but not me. I'm twenty-two, see. I'm twenty-two and about to graduate from college. But you can't see that."

"I don't understand."

"You can't see it for all the fucking layers. All the stuff piled on. Layers of experience. Layers of great stories. Hey, I'll keep you up all night, telling stories. And what do you know at the end of the night? Stories. Layers. Layers of clothing. Layers of fat. Why do people get fatter as they get older, did you ever think about that?"

"No."

"We do it on purpose. Cover up what's really there."

"What's really there?"

Jim took another belt of wine, draining the glass. The alcohol rushed to his brain, unimpeded by those layers of purposeful fat. God, was he really going to tell this little girl everything? On the other hand, why not? "The truth," he answered her. "And the truth is...people don't really change that much. We figure out who we are pretty early, and then spend the rest of our lives covering it over."

"That's sad."

"You can't imagine how sad. I take back what I said about your dad. Maybe he's not old enough. He appears mature and responsible and very much in control but that is probably just a layer called Doctor."

Penultimate caught an errant gust and swung hard against her mooring. Jim felt the boat settle down but he kept swinging. Both he and she (the boat) were straining at the chain. He wanted something to happen that night. Something. Anything.

Susan stood and crossed over to the boat's steering wheel, absent-mindedly flicking the spokes back and forth. Jim smiled inwardly–in situations like this, women were always at the helm, whether they realized it or not. "So, if I ask you something, on your birthday, you've gotta tell me the truth, right?"

"I'll tell you the truth."

"Was it really too rough to pick up my mother on the beach? Or did you just want to be alone with me?"

Jim grinned. "The truth is: neither."

"Neither?"

"To get her in the boat, you know, safely, I would have had to get out on the beach myself and hold the bow for her. And I couldn't do that."

"Why not?"

"Because...because I made a promise to myself, on this trip. I wasn't going to go ashore. Not even touch land once. I was going to float. I needed to float for a while. That's the only reason. I know that sounds stupid."

"You'd be surprised how not stupid it sounds," she replied.

"You said, the kids at your new school looked at you like you were invisible."

"Right through me."

"I can imagine that's very painful when you're sixteen..."

"Seventeen."

"I know it's devastating when you're forty. When you meet someone, maybe a young woman, and...and nothing happens. There is no spark. You're invisible, you're not even there. You're an obstacle to be avoided through adroit conversation."

She came back across the cabin to sit next to him, quite close. "What about your wife? Don't you have kids?"

"They're the best. They come the closest. But sometimes I can't help the feeling that...that the man they love is a few ticks of some atomic clock different from me. Or like, in the movie, when they threw paint on the Invisible Man. Who do you see then–the man, or the paint? It's not true that you acquire more self-knowledge as you get older. You get less. It gets harder and harder to hold onto that guy. Once, when you were young, you knew him. Later, you recall that you met him. By the time you get to be my age, you find yourself searching through old pictures for some evidence, less sure all along that it ever really happened."

Jim stopped talking then. Jesus, what was left to say? He felt drained. But this emptiness lasted all of five seconds, until he turned to look at his shipmate.

She was weeping.

"Susan, please don't."

"It's so sad."

"No, no, it's not so sad. Maybe once a decade I feel like this. Really. And I shouldn't say it's like that for everybody. I don't know if it is or not. Probably not. Come here..."

He put his arm around her and drew her to him. She settled in close to his side and instinctually nestled her leg up over his lap. They were close. He could see the comic fuzz of a young girl's moustache across her upper lip.

"Please don't take to heart the ravings of some confused old man you met, on a stormy night at sea."

"I don't see you as old...or invisible."

"Then, tonight, I'm not." He kissed her lightly on the lips. She kissed him back.

They sat there, silent in half embrace for quite some time as *Penultimate* creaked around her six tons of gravity. Some few minutes after midnight, Susan asked him: "Yesterday, when you sailed up to the island?"

"Right?"

"There was a guy on the deck. He was naked."

"Yeah. That was Gregor, the guy who stepped on the urchin."

"He was shouting something."

"He was?"

"Yeah. What was he saying?"

"Uh...I don't know."

"What was it?"

"I...can't remember."

"What did that guy say?"

Susan's father and Peter returned very early the next morning. It was the sound of the chopper passing over the cove that woke them up. The storm had blown through without incident.

Susan waved to her father from the afterdeck of *Penultimate.* Jim came up through the hatch on *Circe's* foredeck and squinted.

Jim had the sloop rigged and ready to depart as soon as the shore boat brought Peter out to the cove. He was alone. He brought Jim up to date on the recovering Gregor but was more interested in island drama than hospital drama. "The mother was on the land line to shore all night," Peter blurted out. "She told him you were on their boat with their seventeen-year-old daughter, you were in the shower with her, you were taking advantage of her..."

"Bullshit. Let's slip the mooring."

"The doctor wanted you to stay until he got out here. Says he wants to thank you."

"It's not my fault she can't swim."

"Who? The girl?"

"The mother. Look, it was too rough to get the mother off the beach. Susan made me a dinner. We talked for a while and then I rowed back over here."

"No shower?"

"What are you, the FBI? I used their shower. I got hypothermic saving their God damn boat. I ate one of their steaks and drank a bottle of wine. Send me a fucking bill!"

Peter held up his hands for mercy. "Okay, Jim, okay." He went forward to start tugging at the strain-hardened mooring line. Jim started the engine. A few minutes later, *Circe* slipped by the stern of *Penultimate* on her way out of the cove. Susan waved to Jim as he passed. Jim waved back. Over his shoulder, he saw the shore boat approaching again, Dr. and Mrs. Gardner in the bow. In full view of them all, he blew Susan a kiss. He saw her smile as she snatched it, single-handed, from the air.

Peter set the main and jib, Jim killed the engine, trimmed, and then they settled into the cockpit for the passage back. "I'm sorry," Jim said after a few minutes. "I wasn't angry at you."

"It's okay."

"I just know they're going to give her a hard time over this and there's nothing I can do."

"Nice kid?"

"Great kid."

"Well, the doctor's not a bad guy. They won't be so hard on her, when they find out nothing happened." Peter hesitated a moment. "Of course, blowing her that kiss isn't going to help her much."

Jim smiled. "She deserved a kiss."

It was a fast passage back to the mainland in the steady post-storm winds. They alternated steering and napping below; neither had slept much the night before. They were both on deck, however, when *Circe* rounded the last marker and settled down on a course parallel to the beach that would bring her inside the breakwater.

"So, what are the final results?" Peter asked. "Did you beat gravity?"

Jim didn't answer at first. They were thirty or so yards off the surf line. "You can take her in, can't you?" he asked.

"Where the hell are you going?"

"Finish the experiment."

"You're a fucking madman," Peter exclaimed.

Jim stripped to his shorts and catapulted over the rail. The water was unexpectedly cold. He started swimming hard for the beach. There was no current and the breakers were small. The surf rose up in a sharp line and cracked into foam. He stroked a few more yards in the froth, then lowered his landing gear and touched coarse sand.

Undertow tried to reverse him but Jim dug in his toes and clawed toward the beach. Gradually the sea sluiced away from his waist, his thighs, his ankles. He drew free of it, grew light-footed. He trotted up out of the soup, onto dry sand, took a deep breath and looked down the curving potential of beach. In mid-week, in early June, at forty, he had it all to himself.

FOUR MACKEREL, OR WHY I FISH

an essay

It's difficult to get the teenagers up at four a.m. for just about anything and the threadbare novelty of going fishing with Dad is a particularly poor motivator. So by the time we'd put the boat in the water and bounced the eight miles south to Rocky Point, the quality (fisherman code for "big") yellowtail and barracuda which might have been biting at dawn had long since retired.

After two months of summer job, my daughter was bound for freshman year and just wanted to kick back in the bow. But my son wanted to fish, so I rigged up a rockfish gang line with a big weight so he could get the bait to the bottom. A gang line in this context is a series of bait-keeping hooks (four to six) snelled to leaders which themselves branch off from a central heavy line. Sold neatly tacked to a cardboard retainer inside a plastic pouch, once opened they cry yahoo, embrace chaos, and will never again be made to sit in so orderly a fashion. I remember my strange musing when I bought my first packet of this common angling product. "Gang line?" So close in pronunciation to "ganglia," exquisitely sensitive strands of nerve tissue connecting body to brain. Actually this neural reference makes some unintended sense–a tug on any hook is instantly transmitted to the leader, to the master line, and then up to one's sensory thumb where it rests against the line near the reel.

"Bite."

"Set it!"

Chris jerked the rod up. "Another bite. Dad, I think I've got more than one fish on!"

"That's possible. Crank!"

It was, of course, very possible. Fishing with multiple baits often results in multiple strikes. On the fertile rock cod reefs of Morro Bay, on California's Mid Coast, it is quite common to pull up two or three big fish on a single gang line. The angler's jackpot is that cast which produces a vermilion rockfish on a top hook, a gold-colored canary on a middle bait, and a big, dull-green lingcod on the bottom. It's called the traffic light.

We were too shallow for lingers but Chris's suspicion about his catch proved right. He cranked up four Pacific mackerel, one fish for every hook he had offered. The fish were smallish, teenagers themselves. They flipped about in the shallow water next to the boat in an uncomprehending rage, tangling the leaders and lines into a slimy brain teaser knot. Chris was elated. "Four of them!" he cried. "Look! Four on one line!"

Four silver living spearpoints, all muscle and instinct, scintillating in the hated light of day. The Freshman came back from the bow and the three of us observed the four of them for a few moments. Mackerel are good fighters and these four were ideal specimens, figuring in their own clean logic that any problem, any snare can be overcome by a harder tail-kick, a more forceful corkscrew.

They were beginning to hurt themselves in their fury to be free. "Dad, do something," the Freshman demanded. "If you're not going to keep them..."

I practice catch-and-release fishing most of the time. I'll keep a big, meaty halibut and cut the spines right off a sculpin, but mackerel are junk fish. Real fishermen (not that I count myself in that company) might have hauled them aboard as bait for larger prey, but this wasn't the macho run to Todos Santos or San Miguel. Still, I hesitated. There was something about these fish and this event.

"Dad?!" she repeated in a guilt-inducing tone, one she had honed with much practice.

I pulled my fishing pliers and tried to nab the shank of the hook in the uppermost mouth. Their froth of desperation made it nearly impossible. Amazingly, the hooks were set in almost exactly the same position in each of their mouths. They would not be calmed, not by any such alien blandishments as soothing voice or gentle touch. Eventually all four came off clean, hitting the water with an indignant whole-body shudder and gone.

"Yes! Four on one!" Chris exulted. He baited up again right away and dropped to the bottom, trying to repeat the triumph. He never did. The bite actually cooled off after that, the ocean imposing its own limits. Four-on-ones and traffic lights don't pile up in a man's life.

The Freshman returned to sunbathing. But I could not shake the image of those four fish. They had mesmerized me, haunted me. Once before I had been caught in a trance cast by a fish. He had been a Never Die, *Sebastes caurinus*, a variety of rockfish. I pulled this one from a structure spot called Topanga Bubbles. He was legal, fat and the first catch of the day so I put him in the forward locker. I didn't know it at the time but this fish is famous for surviving out of the water; it's how he got the name. All the rest of the morning he banged away with the flat of his tail on the fiberglass sides of the locker. Whack! Whack! Whack! reminding me of his outrage and my trespass. By afternoon the pace of his protest slowed somewhat, but it never stopped. An hour would pass and then: Whack! Ninety minutes later, just as I swore relief at his finally passing: Whack! You asshole. Whack! You killer!

The names I imagined him calling me were not flattering but disrespect usually bounces off. It is those things which alter personal imagery that burrow deep. The late James Dickey wrote an evocative poem titled "Pursuit From Under," in which arctic explorers are pursued by killer whales whose shadows can be seen underfoot, distorted by the "flawed glass" of the ice. Dickey's conceit: These explorers had been given "a vision of how the drowned dead pursue us."

The Topanga Bubbles provided me with a similar vision: This is how our sins pester us, how the spiritual world reminds us of the running total. The Never Die never died. He thumped in the locker all the rest of the day. In the trunk of the car he swished around in the melt water amid unopened cans of beer. At home that night he rustled his newspaper shroud inside the Maytag sarcophagus. Hundreds of miles from the sea and many years later, I still hear his tail in the middle of the night, beating its erratic tattoo against the bulkheads of my complacency.

What was it about four mackerel?

I came to realize…it was their *sameness*. They were entirely, blindingly, stunningly identical. I could not tell one of them from the other. God could not have done so. There was an ineluctable ferocity of design there, an enormously powerful ideal form that had been repeated and reproduced and reaffirmed in one perfect copy after another, forever. These four living things were actually *one* living thing. And as I looked down into their source, the opaque sea, I realized the further truth of it—there were more than four of these perfect creatures. There were thousands, hundreds of thousands, millions beneath our feet. They comprised just one creature, called Mackerel, a massive, shifting, imponderable being. Chris and his baited nerve ending had pulled from it the smallest possible sample, a scale, a cell, from which one could pretend to extrapolate the full design, realizing at the same time that the human brain could never be pounded so thinly as to wrap around the whole of it.

Here is one instance in which the English language gets it right. We catch one fish, then another. Now we have two fish. No distinction—each fish is both singular and plural.

How are we to approach this reality? Can we even begin to reach out with our minds, much vaunted for their empathetic ability, and relate to such an alien concept? What can it possibly be like to be such a creature, to be both singular and plural at the same time? We talk with often overweening pride about the Human Race and our bonding membership in it, but we cannot begin to emulate the bond shared by four mackerel. Surely each fish has a dim, inchoate idea that it is a being separate from its cohort. They must occasionally see one of their number off to the fringe of the school, minutely, momentarily separate. In the precise ballet of the school, surely once in a while there is a miscue. One fish swims by mistake into another; how can separateness be denied at that moment?

Listen to me here, struggling, grasping for speech to describe a creature which, as I experience life, barely qualifies as being alive. Without individuality, without a sense of separate being, the human mind founders; I can't define us without defining me. But it's not the only workable strategy, is it? Damn it if there isn't a certain hard strength in being Mackerel. The tuna, the yellowtail, the sharks and we skiff types have been hunting them for eons and we haven't made a dent. Mackerel are not endangered; they are at their evolutionary summit. Just look at the design, that exquisite scimitar of cartilage called a tail. Look at how their mission is expressed in their bodies, eighty per cent of which is devoted to driving it through the water and zero percent devoted to figuring out where to go. Blissfully immune to the fevers of individuality, they never have to stand up and be counted; their world bears their weight and their numbers are incalculable.

Indeed there may be only one event in the life of a mackerel when the individual is differentiated from the species. I have been hinting at it above, playing pronoun games. Which of our four mackerel was male? Which of them carried eggs? I couldn't tell but presumably *they* could. Doesn't it seem likely that in the sex act, at least, there would be some dim sense that one's mate was different? Differently equipped, with a different agenda? Thus at the very moment that defines the prime work of the species, its genetic survival, the strict solace of the school is stripped away and, fleetingly, one sees oneself as unique and important in the great ocean of things. Talk about coming hard!

So when, if ever, can we fishermen glimpse the mackerel mind? It isn't easy; we are so anti-mackerel. Our lives are spent in a frenetic effort to make ourselves as different from each other as we can be. There is no colder insult than "how ordinary." No rock and roll classics extol a *member* of the Pack. Looking back, from the twenty-first century to the caves of Lascaux, the one inexhaustible human trait is our mania for individuality. All fashion, art, music, literature, education, cuisine, dance, business… everything we do is in service of differentiation. "I think, therefore I am," says the philosopher, meaning "I think my *own* thoughts." Only in times of the greatest national peril do we suppress our mania to be different and put on the uniform. Even then there's Patton.

But if you still want a peek, here is one trivial approach you could try. To understand mackerel. Decide with your best friends that you are going to a nude beach. Plan to go in separate cars and meet up when you get there. Now you're there and you're naked—where are your friends? You can't find them, can you? These are the people you know best in the world, perhaps, but they are utterly indistinguishable from the rest of the fish slow-roasting on the sand. You can't even tell men from women at any distance. You're floating identity-free in a crowd of nudie clones, just the society four mackerel cherish most.

This nude beach experiment might be rendered a little less trivial, however, if we suspend the rules for the afternoon. By that I mean to banish the taboos of society and let everyone have at it–turn the world's least sexy littoral into an orgy. Heedless of convention, or virus, anybody can do it to anybody else. For just this afternoon. Four hours. Go. Wander the blinding sand, groping for partners who appear identical to begin with and who, after some initial excitement, begin to *feel* pretty much the same, too. Absent distinguishing clothing, habits, mannerisms (and no talking either, did I mention that?) how long would it take before you couldn't take it anymore? I'll give you ninety minutes before you're begging partners to put some clothes on and start thinking about dinner.

There's a certain broad irony here. The same act that lifts four mackerel from their anonymity buries us in ours. Because we expect too much of sex? Hell, we expect too much of everything. Everything we do must serve our fanatical, nearly suicidal drive for distinctness. It is an innate form of wishful madness. Dance harder and add more feathers to the headdress—surely the cure must come.

Finally I wonder, as I think of it, if this is the case with all people. Surely there are Buddhist fishermen working the waters, pulling from the depths local versions of Never Die and traffic light. Their spiritual leader teaches that the goal of life is to banish the self, to surrender to the Oneness. They are encouraged to lean into hardship, to be calm and accepting, to expose the core of Being and let those personal spooks (which we are so adept at creating) be flushed out by white wind. Can this be done? Is an enlightened Mackerel-ness attainable by the species that invented the stiletto high heel? I hope so. I'd like to have the option. Because as I tried to shake the hooks from those four blindingly identical mouths, it occurred to me that I was not certain which of these broad pathways (Buddha, mackerel, man) holds the most promise.

People ask me why I fish and I guess this is it. In no other sport (certainly not lethal firearm hunting) do you have the experience of suddenly extracting a creature from an alien world, absorbing all its colors, textures, and social/spiritual strategies in a single fresh moment...and then returning it unharmed to the sea. If on occasion this causes the fisherman to question some rather larger issues, then I guess that is simply another hazard of the sport, like sunburn on an oversized cranium or a hook in the flesh of the opposable thumb.

WISH HARBOR

When you listen to people (and that's mainly what I do), they talk about the ocean with curvy words. Ocean swells are called rollers. Surfers ride tubes, right up onto crescent beaches. Tug is proud when he says he's sailed "all 'round the Pacific." Not back and forth on the same course over and over, wearing a rut in the water, which is what he did, hauling millions of Jap compact cars. "All 'round the Pacific," he says, like he was Captain Cook or something, sailing the great circles.

Where we live is where the ocean turns square and industrial, not a natural curve to be found. The inner basin, where the tuna boats offload, is just a concrete tub three hundred yards on a side and filled with black, greasy fish-gut slop water. Every angle is ninety hard degrees, disgusting corners where the worst of it lingers, rotting. I took my skiff in there once–never again. The smell down next to the waterline was enough to bleach your hair, and with the wakes of the boats rebounding off those concrete walls, it was all I could do to hang on. One hand for the boat, the other for my nose.

Where we live it's a little nicer. Still square, though. The sea wall makes a right turn just behind the marina and connects the Federal Prison with the rest of the world.

People ask if we worry about having the prison so close but we don't. Once a month they blow the sirens for practice and about once every ten years for real. By and large it's pretty quiet in here, in the Outer Basin of Fish Harbor, on the half dozen floating slips where the half dozen of us live, aboard our boats, cheap and under the radar of the city. Fact is, on a bright Sunday when all the dry docks are silent and there's no truck traffic, it's real nice down here, in the square shadows of the bridge.

Everybody was hunkered down in his canoe one rainy Sunday night in March when a pair of headlights turned into the parking lot. Had to be some stranger because every resident knows to kill his lights in the lot. Otherwise the whole marina turns into a police line-up...just the thing some of my tenants are here to avoid.

"Marion!" a voice shouted. Alex I think. Alex was a skin diver by trade, a stoner by profession. Bright lights were not his thing.

"Yeah?" I answered.

"Who's making a movie?"

It was the worst insult in Fish Harbor. We all hated the self-important Hollywood film crews who used our docks for their locations.

At times like these I earn my pay. Into the parka and up through the hatch. Of course I got halfway up the ramp when the headlights backed out onto the street and soothing darkness was restored.

There was someone standing there by the office, drooping in the rain. Small frame, head hanging low at the shoulders.

"Can I help you?" I shouted.

A woman's voice peeped out of the dismal figure. "I…I'm looking for the manager."

"I'm the manager but the office is closed."

"Is there anywhere to get out of the rain?"

"No. You can call the cab back. There's the phone."

That's when I heard a child cry. You don't hear that much in Fish Harbor. There are a few pleasure sailors who rent cheap slips. Weekends they'll bring their families. It's nice to hear kids laughing and having a good time. This one wasn't.

The woman was huddled under the meager overhang of the marina office, using her back to provide a little more shelter for two very young children. Three years old and six, maybe. None of them had rain gear worth a damn.

"I didn't know you had kids," I said.

The woman didn't look much older than a teenager herself. She was very thin, pale-faced except for the light blue around her wildly chattering lips. "We….we…" she tried to speak.

I unlocked the door to the office and settled them all down in front of the one space heater. It took forever for the pathetic wires to start glowing. "Thank you, thank you so much," the young mother was finally able to say. "We, we came right from the airport. The taxi driver…he had a hard time finding this place."

"They mostly do."

"It took all my cash. I don't have any money for…for a ride anywhere." She rubbed the hands and feet of her children. "How are my babies? Better now, right?" They were too tired or cold to answer. They had that look that kids get when they pull it all in and just try to get through the pain. The woman had it, too.

"I'm sorry I was rude before," I said. "I'm Marion Hart."

"Patti Dell, from Indiana. Has anybody been asking for me?"

"Here? In Fish Harbor? No. You meeting somebody?"

"I...I, yeah. I mean, he was supposed to bring a boat."

"A boat?"

"For us to live in. People live here. On boats, right?"

"Yeah, but..."

"Momma, I'm hungry," the little girl said. No whining, real grown up.

"I don't have anything, honey. Tomorrow we can...."

"You don't have to wait," I told the little girl. "Come over here and see what you want."

I run a little concession out of the office. A pair of glass-front coolers with various stuff people might want. One cooler is all beer. In the other I have some of those sandwiches in the triangle plastic, you know. Made God knows when, but these babies were really cold and hungry. I popped two "Hoagies" in shrink wrap into the old microwave. The kids watched the carousel plate turn round and round inside.

"I'll have to pay you tomorrow," Patti said.

"Tomorrow's soon enough. You want a beer?"

"I'd love one."

We popped a couple tops together. "Welcome to California," I said.

She slipped off her big-ass raincoat. My first impression was right. She was as skinny as a bamboo gaff and looked about like a teenager, a dirty, confused one. She looked tired, too, real sitting-up-in-the airport tired. When the microwave beep went off, her kids tore into those steaming fake-meat logs like wolves. "Hungry," I said.

"Kevin, Natalie, say thank you to Mrs. Hart."

"Thank you," came the sweetest voices. Real gratitude, too, not some mommy-says etiquette. I loved those kids from the first minute. Not a peep, not a whimper of complaint out of 'em. Strong and simple and loyal. The boy pushed part of his sandwich toward his mom. "No, honey," she said. "You finish it. I'm too..." She looked at me, not fetching up the word. "I can't eat."

I asked her a little more about this boat that was supposedly coming but she was too exhausted to talk. She did ask if maybe she and the kids could spend the night in the office; they could just curl up next to the heater. Damn if I was gonna let that happen, not when I'd been keeping an eye on old Frischmann's Chris Craft for six months. All the times I'd opened her up and aired her out and checked his trickle-charger, for free? I figured that added up to a couple nights of frequent flying. So when they finished the Hoagies I helped them move into Frischmann's canoe. Those babies saw that big v-berth forward, stumbled into it and were gone to Dreamland.

Patti Dell stood in the dripping companionway, just looking up at me. A little girl face and big sunk-down eyes. She had something on her mind, I could tell, but it just came out simple: "Thanks."

Nobody much liked Frischmann. He was a big shot mechanical expert, made big money flying all over the world fixing rocket engines or something. And tight with a buck? He could have had a condo or a house, like most of us dream of doing, but he lived aboard to scrimp the last dime. Never did fit in, so nobody minded that I let Patti Dell from Indiana and her kids live on his boat for a couple of days. They fit in better than he ever did.

It doesn't take much to fit in around here–it ain't exactly high society. At that time there were five regulars, not counting me. There was Alex the stoner diver and his partner, Harmon. They lived on a crusty old Hatteras 32 that hadn't left the slip in twenty years. Did mostly hookah dives around the marina, cleaning bottoms for other people who never moved their boats. Sucking air through hoses all day, sucking smoke through hoses all night.

There was Hanks, the vet. He was in his fifties, walked with a pair of canes and lived on a Catalina 25. How any full-grown man lived in a space that small I'll never know. But Hanks was a master at keeping things simple. I went aboard once, when he was down with the flu and I was worried about him. An amazingly tidy and organized space, made his 25 look bigger than my 38.

On the big Carver 45 at the end tie is Mr. Karandas. Nice fellow, got some bucks, mainly because he works so hard at that restaurant of his. It's a sort of Greek and Mediterranean place in Pedro, across the bridge. There's a standing invitation for any of us harbor folks to have a half-price meal over there. I went once and it was damn good. Karandas is friendly but kind of a loner. You can hear him playing that Greek mandolin at night on his afterdeck. I heard somewhere that he lost his family in a war over there. That makes sense.

Last, there was Danny, our miracle man. A miracle he was still alive, chain-smoking at four hundred pounds. A miracle that his boat didn't sink right out from under him. It wasn't more than an old Skipjack 26 he called *Lisa*, with Danny, all of him, plopped down permanently in the portside settee, sending her into a perpetual list. But it was Danny's *Lisa* that was the most active boat in the harbor. Every other day, good weather or bad, you could count on Danny to fire up the old Volvo diesel and cast off the kelp beds. He'd pick up bait at the barge and limp out past the Federal Breakwater into the Pacific, heeled way over like a boat that's sinking. A miracle, too, that he came back every time…and every time he came back with fish. Rockfish, bonito, yellowtail, even tuna in the Nino years. He knew the spots and he knew the fish. He was skunk-proof.

He always had clouds of gulls following him in from the sea. Before long little Kevin and Natalie Dell became like those birds, waiting with bright, hungry eyes for Big Dan to return. They'd fall in behind his heavy steps as he hauled his catch up the ramp to our little picnic area. Danny told them all about the red-orange and dark green fish, their names and what they like to eat. Then he proved he knew what he was talking about by gutting the fish out and showing what was in their bellies. Those kids weren't in the least bit squeamish. They thought Danny was magic.

Pretty soon the smell of charcoal-roasting fish spread over the docks and we all emptied out of our canoes for dinner. Everybody who showed up got to share, even Frischmann when he was in town. All Danny ever asked in return was maybe you picked him up a couple of cartons at the store when his feet were hurting.

It was simple, it was neighborly. It was the way things worked, up 'til then.

Maybe about a week after they moved in, I was walking past Frischmann's boat about eight or so. Must have been bedtime for the babies because I saw them playing around in their jammies on the afterdeck. Mighty cute, those two. A moment later out came Patti. She gathered them up and they all went forward, to the open bow. The kids got real calm, serious. "Okay," Patti said, "say good night to Daddy."

They looked out and up toward the sky a little, and waved their hands. "Good night, Daddy."

"Night, Daddy."

"Night."

My Tug was dozing late one morning, after one of our little "sleepovers." He's not the prettiest man in the world, especially when he's snoring, so I don't watch. I walked up the dock and was just putting the key in the office door lock when the phone started to ring.

"Fish Harbor Marina."

"Yeah, yeah, Fish Harbor. Is that you?"

"This is the marina office. Who do you want to…"

The man's voice was solid with impatience and anger. "Look the fuck out at the water, do you see me out here?"

I looked. In the middle of the channel was a classic trawler, maybe 36 feet, brown hull, white trim. A guy was standing at the flying bridge. He gave a short, pissed-off wave.

"Can you fucking see me?"

"Yeah, I see you."

"Okay. Where's Patti Dell?"

"Patti? What do you want Patti for?"

"This is her god-damned boat! Where am I supposed to put it?"

Patti had told me again that she was expecting a boat to be delivered for her and the kids to live on, but I didn't pay it much mind. You hear a lot of pipe dreams.

"Wait a minute," I said as I reached up for the dock master's book. That trawler was beamy, with a long bow-sprit. It wouldn't fit just anywhere.

"Come one, come on, I got things to fucking do."

"You're going to be out there all day if you don't learn some manners. Can you still see me?"

"Yeah."

"Follow where I walk. I'll put you in D-14."

The next half-hour was pure comedy. There is nothing that boat people like better than watching somebody try to handle a vessel when they really don't have a clue. This bozo had given away any clues he was born with. One by one people poked their heads out to watch the show. It was dead calm and he still couldn't line the trawler up for a run at the slip. He came in sideways, he came in diagonal, he came in so crooked it was almost backwards. Which would have worked if he understood the throttles at all. But the trawler was lurching forward when it should have been creeping and then foaming in reverse with the helm hard over the wrong way. He couldn't do anything right, to the enormous amusement of Tug, Danny, Alex and the rest. Worse, he could hear them laughing and rage made him even stupider.

"God damn this thing!" came the epithets across the water.

"Is that our boat?" Kevin asked his mother.

"It's going to be," Patti replied, "I hope."

The humor went out of it all of a sudden when the idiot came within a red hair of slamming into Mr. Karandas's *Helen*. "Tug," I pleaded, "take the skiff and give the man a hand."

"Aw, Jeez, Marion, I'm off duty."

"Aw, Jeez, Tug."

He pulled on a shirt, launched the skiff and sculled out to the trawler. Some pretty hot language was exchanged before he got the guy to stand away from the helm and let him take over. Within five minutes Tug had her snugged down in D-14. "What an asshole," he confided to the world. "Total fucking asshole," he repeated to the man's face before clumping off down the dock.

Total Fucking Asshole wasted no time getting off the trawler. He spotted Patti and the kids. "You gotta be her. Let's get this over with." He pulled a series of papers out of a black metal briefcase and almost threw them in her face. The boat was hers, paid in full. Insurance too, paid up for a year; after that, she'd have to pay for it herself. Plus five hundred dollars in cash, "to feed the brats." There was only one condition: Patti had to keep the boat in working order. "Start the fucking engine every now and then, and don't let things rot." That was it, the Asshole had done his part and he wanted out of this "fucking piss-hole." He made a quick call on his cell phone as he stalked off toward the parking lot.

"Nice," I complimented her on her new home.

"Yeah," she said, permitting a rare smile.

"And free, too," I added.

It seemed like she was going to say something, but she didn't. Silence hung in the air for a moment. Then she said: "We've got business to do, right? A lease to sign?"

"Right."

"I'll come up to the office later."

Patricia Bauer Dell was her full name. The boat was nameless and that's what I wrote in the space, *No Name.*

"It's perfect," she agreed.

The ownership papers were in order, the prior owner being somebody named Medina. Patti said she wanted a six month lease, just a slip with electrical power, no phone line, no maintenance. I took it all down and gave her what she asked for, but my concerns were building up pretty fast. I don't pry, you know, but here was this young woman with these two sweet babies. "Patti, you know, the five hundred he gave you is not going to last very long. You can ride with me to Fedmart and buy cheap, but even then..."

"I've got to get a job."

"But you don't have a car."

"Something I can walk to, then."

"Well, that's pretty limited around here. You can't work on the fish line; they won't let you, it's all Asians. Maybe the prison is hiring."

"No."

"What about your babies? What will they be doing while you're at work?"

She hung her head and shook it slowly. She hadn't thought much about this.

"The Marina can be dangerous for kids."

"They both swim like fish."

"This is not the pool at the YMCA. They could fall under a boat or a dock. I can't watch 'em all the time."

"I'm not asking you to. I can take care of things." It was the first time I'd heard her be assertive. "You don't hear me complaining," she went on. "I liked our old house as much as anybody. But this is where we're living now. Somebody gives you a free house," she said, gesturing to the no-name boat, "and you take it, even if it doesn't have a lawn and backyard swings and a nice car in the garage. Or a toilet or a sink. So they wash and brush with a cup of water every night and pee in a bottle. It's been done before. Lots of people."

"You're right," I agreed. As she went back to reading and signing the lease documents, I offered: "I don't mind keeping an eye on them, as much as I can. They're really sweet babies. I love the way they say good night, to their daddy." Patti looked up at me. "He's gone, is he?" I asked.

"Yes."

"I'm sorry."

I offered to help her move aboard *No Name* but she said it would be good for the kids to move their own things. A few days later they invited folks over for a little boat-warming party. It was fun. There was lots of beer (courtesy of me) and fish tacos (Danny). Everybody brought some little gift. Alex and Harmon brought Kevin a cut-down diver's mask, which he loved. Nick Karandas gave Natalie a kind of Greek flute with a little wooden ball floating inside it. Books, plates, fenders, little stuff Patti needed.

I took a chance and gave her something useless, a really nice Kukui nut necklace Tug had brought me from Hilo years ago. He's brought a lot more souvenir stuff since (hell, I've been dating the guy for fifteen years), so I gave this one to Patti. She really liked it, put it on right away and it matched up real nice with the dark red dress she was wearing.

You know, I don't pretend to understand men. To me, Patti looked real nice that day, with the short-cut dress and her hair all clean and fresh cut. Okay, so she didn't have any make-up on and she was kind of thin and hungry-looking, with Kevin welded to her hip most of time. I guess I can understand why the guys weren't jumping all over her. They had their own handicaps, too: Alex and Harmon too stoned, Danny too fat, Nick too sad. Tug bolted to me. But all the time Patti lived here, none of the guys ever really tried to get close to her. Of course, what happened next had a lot to do with that. And this story isn't about men, anyway: It's about women and I do understand women. Even if in the end, even if still today, I didn't know for sure about everything that happened.

Nick had taken Natalie up to the bow, away from the chatter, to practice the flute. "What thit called?" she asked with her small child's lisp.

"A Santorini Flute," the restaurateur answered. "From the islands of Greece."

"Fwum islands of Gweese," she repeated.

"Yes. I lived near a harbor there once. Now I live in a harbor here."

"Wish Harbor."

"Yes, Wish Harbor."

Patti Bauer Dell, single mom from Indiana living on a no-name cruiser in slip D-14, picked up the rhythms of life in the Marina pretty quick. You could tell because she could tell—if a halyard broke free on one of the sailboats and started swinging, if the sea lions started piling up where they shouldn't, if Danny switched from port side to starboard—she noticed, just as sure as one of us old-timers would.

"What's that?" she asked one day in early summer, pointing out into the channel.

"I don't know," I answered.

She was just coming home after her half-day at the dry docks. She had found a part-time job there, clerking for the Personnel Manager. She started real early in the a.m., leaving her kids still asleep in the forward cabin and walking across the road to the yard. When Kevin and Natalie woke up, they knew to come up to the office for some breakfast and cocoa. I'd watch 'em for most of the morning. Or if I had to go somewhere, they'd go tag along after Alex, or Danny would read to them. We managed—they were never unsupervised for very long.

"Just showed up last night," I continued. "If it's there tomorrow, I'll take a row out."

We were talking about a pretty nice canoe, a brand-new Carver 38 Special, gleaming with chrome and decked out with fresh blue canvas covers to match its dark blue hull. Every conceivable kind of up-link, antenna, and reflector sprouted from the stubby electronics mast amidships and an FOB French Avon inflatable, bright red, was tethered to her stern alongside a sea kayak. A big, beautiful package, three to four hundred grand worth of boat, tenders and gear, tied to a rusty, gull-shit covered mooring buoy in Fish Harbor? It was a mystery.

Later that afternoon, Patti and the kids were over at Nick's. She had a kind of second job for him, cleaning his boat and doing some of the restaurant's bookwork. She told Nick that her husband had been an accountant and she knew a little about withholding and W-2's, all of which (he actually said) was Greek to him. Patti had the kids helping her on the foredeck, polishing bright work, when she looked up at the approaching sound of a small outboard. It was the red Avon from the new cruiser, coming in for a landing at the marina office dock. At the tiller was a striking young woman, her lean legs tanned and bare, her upper torso sheathed in a sexy sleeveless wetsuit top in the same color as the inflatable. She was tall and thin, a model's figure, really, and her white-blonde hair had a close-cropped, saucy look to it. The woman smiled at the kids and waved. They just stared back, the three of them, polishing rags in hand. They weren't being unfriendly, they just couldn't believe their eyes. Even children knew: This kind of bird did not nest in Fish Harbor.

"Hello?" The woman announced her presence at the Marina office. Up close you could see the Norway, or maybe Iceland, in her forceful, perfect face and glacier blue eyes.

"Can I help you?"

"Hi. My name is Liz. Elizabeth Thorsen. I'm on the boat that's tied up out there, the blue hull?"

"Uh, yeah, we noticed you. Somebody owns that mooring, you know."

She smiled even more broadly, reassuring and, I gotta say, enchanting. "Oh yes, I know him. I have his permission."

She reached up under the bottom edge of the wetsuit vest and pulled out a rounded oblong of black plastic. At one corner was an inflation stub, which she twisted, permitting air to rush out. Then she ran her fingers along one edge and, with a *scratch* of Velcro, the oblong opened up into a document pouch. It was black nylon inside and very hi-tech. I'd never seen one like it. That was Liz, as I came to know her—everything the most modern and most expensive.

She showed me a copy of the lease agreement for the mooring, which I compared to the original on file in the office. Identical, leased to Lawrence Knowles. She also had a 'to whom it may concern' on his letterhead, granting her the use of the boat and the mooring on an indefinite basis. It all checked out.

"So, you'll be living out there?" I asked cautiously.

"Living and working."

"Alone?"

"Only me, from over the sea. You've got families living here, that's nice."

"Just Patti and her kids. What kind of work?"

"Survey."

"Surveying what?"

The bright face darkened a bit. "It's kind of confidential."

"Sure, okay. Nobody's big on details around here. Kinda day to day."

"That'll be great. I'm sorry, what was your name?"

"Marion."

"Nice to meet you."

"We've got a fish fry going a couple nights a week. You're welcome."

"Okay, okay, maybe I will. Thanks."

On her way back out to the blue-hulled cruiser she waved at the kids again. This time they waved back. Patti just stared. Liz Thorsen also passed Danny coming back in with his day's catch. The sight of her so distracted him that he ran smack into a shoal marker.

As Danny gutted his fish, as he filleted them out, as Alex and Harmon got the coals started, as Hanks shucked corn, as they ate, as they cleaned up and as they lingered past dark with beers and a quart of tequila, Liz Thorsen was all they could talk about. Two dozen times they asked me and two dozen times I told them: "I don't know. She's here to survey, that's all she said."

And I'd bet a month's salary, grand as it is, that after they broke up and went back to their dark canoes, there was more than one pair of binoculars dragged out of jumbled cabinets and aimed over at Liz Thorsen's boat, where a lone cabin light glowed. Even Patti, who had been quiet during the fish fry, stayed out on deck for a while after her kids had said goodnight to Dad, keeping an eye on the new arrival. Yeah, something hypnotic had been dropped into our midst. Danny said it best, a few days later: This must be what it's like when a chrome lure hits bottom and finds a stray beam of light in the murk.

All right, I said what I mostly do is listen but I'm curious, too. I'm not one of these women with a cell phone in each hand, desperate to keep the rumors flowing, but I like to know things about people, especially if they're living in my Marina.

Liz Thorsen remained a blank, a pretty blank, for quite a while. Nobody knew anything about her. For one thing, she rarely came ashore. You could see her in the Avon, running round the corner to Pedro for groceries, or in her kayak, paddling into industrial backwaters, taking samples of water and slime. She seemed to follow no set pattern. The boat would be gone for a whole day, then remain unmoving for a week. She was out in the kayak at all hours of the day and night. At twilight and on into the night, several hours at a time, you could hear her out there playing some kind of wooden flute. Pleasant but aimless melodies, sort of Indian or Irish, I don't know, hours of it.

Everybody noticed her. Hundreds of eyes followed her everywhere she went: guys on the trawlers and long-liners, gutters and shredders in the Harbor, Coast Guard boys from the base across the inlet. It was hard to ignore her.

It brought me one cash benefit. Hard-hats working the dry dock usually ate off the roach coaches that worked the harbor lunch trade. But with Liz out in her kayak or working on the deck of the blue cruiser, they started hanging out at our little Marina picnic area, hogging the tables marked "For Marina Tenants Only."

"We're watching the Little Mermaid," they openly admitted. It was amazing: a ninety-minute lunch break filled with nothing but lewd appraisals of one skinny girl that none of them had even *seen* close up, including the inevitable boasts about what they were going to do when "Ariel grew some legs." Naturally, "bitch" was every other word.

I thought she should know so I told her about her mob of rough admirers. She just smiled and said, "Okay, thanks." Of course she knew already. A girl like that knows everybody's watching her and always has been.

But here's the point of it: She and Patti became friends. Me, I missed it at first. I wouldn't have thought they'd find much in common. What did they, I ask you? Widowed, struggling Patti, devoted to her two kids, scratching out a living doing odd jobs, with her one good red dress and her leaking boat. And Liz Thorsen, the princess? Supported, no doubt, by some merman-king-daddy somewhere. Beautiful and secure and swimming free. An enchantress, who knew it.

They were together a lot. Liz's Avon was tied up alongside the No-Name many hours over the weekends as the two of them sat on deck, talking or doing things with the kids. When Patti's hours at the breaking yard were expanded, the problem of child care was solved by Liz

Thorsen, who took charge of them for several hours in the afternoon. They would spend a lot of time on her boat, which those kids seemed to love. A lot of times Liz would let loose the mooring and take the kids out for a day's romp on the water. Danny said he saw them a lot, when he was out fishing. They'd be on their way over to the Queen Mary or idling along the kelp beds looking for sea lions. Sometimes Patti would come back from work and her kids would still be gone with Liz and then, bless her heart, she actually got a half hour or so for herself. She'd climb up into a hammock on the foredeck and swing there without a care for a little while, going right to sleep. Then there'd come a cry across the water or a short beep on the Avon's horn and Ariel would bring the babies back to her, bursting with some adventure to share.

Liz always seemed to have time to spare; a lot of the survey she was doing seemed to be going on at night, when she'd slide off silently in the kayak and disappear into the dark corners of the harbor. She was SCUBA certified (I could have guessed) and she spent one weekend under the hull of No-Name, scraping off tons of accumulated growth. The kids followed her every move, endlessly fascinated by her bubbles and by the barnacles and worms and limpets she brought up for them to see.

"Eewww! That was growing on our boat?"

"A whole tribe of them," Liz teased from the water line.

Liz cinched down the mask to fit Patti's narrow face and let her use the tanks. Patti came up sputtering and amazed.

"What'd you see, Momma?"

"It's a whole other world."

"What's it like, Momma?"

"It's like you're flying. It's like you're free."

The only problem with that was that it's kind of an unspoken rule around here that Alex is the diver. If your hull needs cleaning, he's the guy that does it. It keeps him and Harmon in work. I mentioned it to Patti once, just in the friendliest way. The next day, Alex tells me, he's coming up to the surface alongside a sailboat job and there's every inch of Liz Thorsen standing next to him on the dock. She wanted to make things right by asking him to scrape the hull of her boat.

Alex said he'd row out the next day and take a look. Which he did and found her hull as clean as the day it popped out of the mold.

Nothing to clean, he told her.

She said she wanted to pay him anyway.

He said that wasn't the way he ran things. If he didn't earn it he didn't want the money.

"She gave me the strangest look," Alex told a bunch of us later, "like I wasn't speaking English or something."

"Of course, I did accept the blow job."

You know men—he had to say it.

The days started getting longer and warmer and more of us were hanging out on deck in the evening. Nobody would admit it, especially not those guys who get all the "blow jobs," but when the sun went down, we all looked forward to it. I mean the little ritual that had become part of life in Fish Harbor, when Kevin and Natalie would climb up on the bow of *No Name* and say good-night to their daddy. I know how I felt about it: like it was a real privilege I'd been given, at my age, with the choices I've made in life, to be able to see such a sweet offering every night. It's like that corner of the roof that's been nothing but trouble for a dozen years, collecting leaves and causing leaks, and then one spring all of a sudden there's eggs in there, and then baby birds. Nobody's immune to this kind of stuff. There's nobody who doesn't want those chicks to make it, to grow up and fly away. There's nobody who doesn't worry about snakes crawling into the nest.

One Sunday afternoon I was trying to catch up on paperwork in the office when the phone rang. It was Patti calling, saying she was going to be late getting home and would I ask Liz to put the kids to bed for her. I said sure, I'd tell her, but just then the prison let loose with a blast on the escape siren. Wake the dead loud, that thing is. I shouted over the noise but I couldn't tell if she heard me. There was something strange about that call, too, but I couldn't quite say what at the time. When the blast was over Patti had hung up.

About dusk Liz came in the Avon with the babies and I told her. "They can stay with us until she gets back," I offered.

"Oh, no, that's okay. I don't mind. I've got plenty of room." She told Kevin and Natalie the plan and they seemed very content as the Avon skittered back to Liz's big-dollar canoe.

Tug came over later with some steaks. After dark I was in the galley doing the dishes when I heard him say "Hi" from topside.

"Hi, Tug. Is Marion around?"

I came up on deck and saw Patti standing next to the boat. Tug said, "Patti, come and have a drink with us."

And she said "Yeah, okay," and came aboard. "Thanks." I don't think I'd ever seen her drink anything but beer before but she bit into the tumbler of scotch pretty deep. She sat right down, too, looking tired and kind of on edge.

"Liz has got the kids, like you said."

"Thanks. Thanks, I appreciate it. I...I appreciate everything, you know. I don't think I say that enough."

"No problem, honey. Is anything wrong? You sounded strange on the phone today."

"No, everything's fine. But I was wondering, Marion, if I could move *No Name.*"

"Move her? Where to? You got a primo berth right now." It was true. The closer-in berths were the sought-after ones. Not so far to trot, you know.

"I was thinking something further out. Away from the noise. Like out here. Closer to Liz. And you, too," she quickly added.

"Well, I...I don't know."

"She can make it happen, honey," Tug butted in. "She's the Queen."

"Liz is only temporary out here, you know that."

Patti smiled, a mommy smile, full of reassurance. "Oh, she'll be here a long time. Her work isn't even started yet. Liz'll be around."

"You've got a real good friend there," Tug said. "The way she pitches in, watching those kids for you."

Her smile changed again. Bigger, prouder. She was talking about her friend Liz. "She's the best. She's been just about everywhere, you know." Patti slugged back a big swallow of the scotch. It warmed her up immediately. "Been all over the east coast and the South. Remember when that big hurricane hit Florida..."

"Andrew?"

Patti nodded. "Liz was living in a house right along a river. On stilts. And the water came up right to the floor. Then she went down to Cuba for a while. We're not sup-posed to go there, you know. Americans aren't. But she was with a Venezuela guy and she met Castro and everything. She's always doing these special projects for people. Like studies. There was a cabin she lived in up in the Rocky Mountains, way up in the rocks, where this professor who owned it was counting...something. That's where she met the people who were training for Aconcagua. That's the tallest mountain in South America."

"She climbed it?"

"Not all the way to the top. Base camp. She sort of ran it for them. She's really amazing." A conspiratorial look fell across her excited face. "I'll tell you something if you promise not to tell." Tug and I nodded. "Last week, she took me with her, on one of her research runs."

"Research runs?"

"Into the inner harbor. We got all dressed in black and rubbed stuff on our faces, just like commandos in movies. We took her raft in partway and then cut the motor and drifted. They never knew we were there."

"Who never knew?" Tug asked.

"The crews. The tuna fish crews, on the boats in there. Liz's got this camera that shoots in the dark. Infra-red. I rowed and she took pictures. Of all the boats. If they seen us, who knows what woulda happened. But she was so good at it, in and out, not a sound, like a pro, with all the evidence. It was real exciting; I really loved it."

"Evidence of what?" Tug asked.

"I...I'm not sure. There's supposed to be, like, a door in the nets, to let the dolphins out."

"Right, the dolphin vent. It's been the law since 1985."

"She checks that. And, like, what's in the water. We took samples. All environmental stuff. She's like a safeguarder."

"I see," Tug replied. He took a long pull on his drink and shut up.

Patti kept going. "Free to go wherever she wants, where she's needed. It's quite a life, huh? One duffle bag. Pack it up and off for adventure." Patti paused and finished her drink in a single slug. "Just the opposite of me," she added.

I couldn't see Patti too well in the darkness but I heard her voice flatten out as she made the inevitable comparison. I had nothing to say. Any woman would feel kind of plain-wrap next to Liz.

"Well, thanks," Patti said after a few moments of silence. As she stood up she asked, "Marion, could I use your skiff to go collect my little things?"

I said sure and off she went, across the water toward the dark shape of Liz's boat.

Later Tug and I were about to go to sleep, both just lying there, thinking about things. About the same thing, it turned out. "She's sure in love with that Lizzy."

"She's not in love," I snapped back. "Is that what you think, it's some lesbian thing?"

"It's not? Too bad," he teased.

I gave him the elbow. "She just admires her."

"I admire Kobe Bryant but I'm not gushing on for ten minutes about how wonderful he is."

"Men and women are different."

"They are?" he teased again.

"Men are all competition and envy. You admire Kobe but I also hear you screaming that nobody is worth that kind of money. Women? Sure, there's lots of jealousy, but it's also possible...I don't know...when somebody does something wonderful, if you're her friend, it's sort of like it happened to you, too. A man'd say: 'That lucky son-of-a-bitch.' But Patti'd say: 'Wow, isn't she something?'"

Tug rolled over in the dark and looked at me. "Did you ever have a friend like that?"

"Me?" I thought a minute. "No. But I understand it."

Tug grunted, but not in an unkind way, then said, "Good night."

"Tug, can I ask you one last thing?"

"Sure."

"It's gonna sound silly."

"Go on."

"If I'm on the phone with somebody and I hear, like, a horn go off on their end, and then a few seconds later I hear the horn myself, just normal, through the air, that means that person is closer to the horn than me, right?"

"Right."

"Where the fuck is my boat?"

I had my back to the counter putting fresh brews in the refrigerator when he pushed the sliding glass open and swore at me. I stood up and looked him over slowly. I remembered him. I felt like messing with him. "What boat are you talking about?"

"The boat I brought in here four months ago. I put it right there." He pointed to the slip where Patti had been before she moved.

Had it really been four months? I paused, making him wait. "No," I finally said, "the way I remember it, somebody had to put it in the slip for you."

"Yeah, and all you fucking losers loved it, too. So where is it?"

"Where's what?"

"My boat."

"That boat belongs to Patti Dell."

"You shouldn't believe everything you read, Grandma."

"You shouldn't believe your own bullshit, Sonny."

"Fuck you."

It felt good to tweak the idiot but the next minute I realized I'd made a mistake. I had pissed the guy off and now he was loping down the ramp to the slips, determined to find *No Name* in a really foul mood. I should have gone with him, showed him the way, 'cause then I could have maybe given Patti some warning.

Anyway, the guy didn't stay very long, no more than twenty minutes. It was ten minutes after that I saw Patti coming up the ramp herself, holding a cloth to the side of her head.

"I need a bag of ice, Marion."

"Jesus, Patti!"

I could see a big cut and spreading bruise under the cloth. Her face was tight with pain and anger, some of it directed at me. "I need a bag of ice and no questions. Please!"

"What happened? Where are the kids? Did they see this?"

But Patti was not Patti right then. She used no words. She slapped the price of a small bag, three faded dollar bills, on the counter with a furious impact. When I still hesitated, she slapped them down again harder. That got her the bag, with no questions.

It's hard to tell about people, even people you see every day. One person could say "No questions" and really mean it, while somebody else is really asking you to ask. That guy had beaten Patti up and if she didn't want to talk about it, then fine. Fish harbor is not a religious retreat where you expect to hear a lot of public confession. Still, I did think it was my obligation, as a sort of friend, to at least ask one more time.

The way Patti had acted, I didn't think I'd have much success asking her all by myself. So that was why, the rest of that day and into the night, I stayed up in the office and watched the outer channel with my binoculars. We had all seen Liz leave her cruiser in the Zodiac late in the morning, loaded up with gear, off on one of her eco-excursions. I waited for her to return. Just after dusk I had seen the babies say goodnight to their daddy and seen the lights in the kids' forward cabin wink out. The lights remained on in the main cabin. I could imagine Patti in there, putting the last of the melting ice to her face. I wanted to go down right then, but I waited. When I finally saw Liz motoring into the channel toward her boat, I ran down to my skiff and rowed out as hard as I could. I intercepted Liz in mid-channel and told her what had happened. Together we made our way over to *No Name* and tied up alongside.

"Patti? Patti, we're not going away."

When there was no answer, Liz called out again. I rapped my knuckles on the solid fiberglass of *No Name*. That brought her bursting out of the companionway.

"Shut up! Banging on the hull, you're going to wake them up."

"I'll stop banging if you come out here and talk to us."

"I got nothing to say."

"Please, Patti," Liz pleaded. "We want to help."

"You can't help. It's just the way things are."

"It's the way what things are?"

"Tell me his name and I'll call the cops," I offered.

I hit the nerve without knowing it. Patti's mouth curled into an ironic grin as she touched the swollen side of her face. She glanced one last time into the cabin to be sure the kids were asleep, then climbed out of the companionway and slid the hatch shut behind her. "Call the cops," she repeated with bitter amusement as she sank into a cockpit seat.

Liz and I settled into the seats on either side of her. Out here, in the dull yellow light of the Marina's sodium vapor lamps, her bruised face looked deathly discolored. "Why did he hit you?"

"You remember the day he delivered this boat?"

"No," Liz answered.

"I do," I said at the same time.

"The only thing he wanted, the one condition was that I kept it in good condition. Made sure the engine would start, that it was able to sail."

"You haven't started that engine the whole time you've been here." It was true. When we had moved *No Name* to the slip next to mine, we tried to start the engine but with no luck. Alex and Hanks finally had to tow her out there with skiffs.

"I know. I should have kept it up. It's my mistake. So, when he came by, it was to check up on all that. When the engine wouldn't turn over, he punched me. That's all."

"You didn't make a mistake," Liz defended her. "It's your boat, you can do what you want with it."

You'd think Patti would agree but she didn't say anything. "It is your boat, right?" I asked.

Patti gave me a hard stare. "It's mine. You saw the papers."

"I saw a boat change hands but not any money."

The stare softened. More than her stare, really, her whole body sort of lost its fiber. Patti Dell had always been pretty tightly wound. Most people wrote it off to the huge load she carried: single mother, living in a tiny space, dirt poor, scratching at odd jobs, but now it was clear that there was something more. When she deflated that night, when all that iron inside melted and ran out of her, it was pretty amazing. I'd seen something like it five years ago, when Tug's cousin was on the crew of that tuna boat that sank off Mexico. It wasn't until they got back, until they were sitting in a bar in Pedro, that they could accept the fact that they had made it, that they could talk about it and not tempt fate. These weren't real chatty guys, you know what I mean, but that night they talked and talked until they had told everything.

Except those guys ended up bragging drunk. Patti Dell just seemed blank, more or less empty. "It is mine. It is. He gave it to me."

"The guy who hit you?"

"No, my husband."

"Before he died."

"He's not dead. I saw him last week."

"Last Sunday," I added. Things were beginning to sort out for me.

"Yes," Patti said simply, "that's right." She turned to Liz as she made her full disclosure. She'd told the lie to both of us but it was Liz's friendship, more than mine, that Patti Dell wanted to soothe with the truth.

Her name was Patti Dell but she was not a widow. She was from Wisconsin, not Indiana. Her husband, Peter, had been an officer with a suburban bank until it was bought out by a large national. There was some concern about his job until Peter got the word that he had been selected by the new bosses for "grooming." Then the trips to California began; the new national headquarters was in Los Angeles. He was gone weeks at a stretch and returned, it seemed to Patti, a little more changed each time.

"What was going on?" Liz asked in a voice very unlike her own, a voice tight with suspicion and cynicism.

"It wasn't 'grooming,' I can tell you that." To use corporate jargon, Peter Dell had been "deselected" early in the process. Fired, let go, downsized. But in California he had met some people on the fringes of the banking industry. Professional depositors, you might call them. Guys who specialized in unrounded amounts and always just under ten thousand.

Peter sent pictures back: the modest one-bedroom in Burbank, the bright-eyed trainee in his black suit, the lonely guy walking the beach–"Miss you, wish you were here." Except just out of frame was the new car, the long weekends spent in Malibu, the California girls. And the boat, the 36-foot trawler now called *No Name*. It was a solid, mainstream kind of vessel that didn't stand out in a crowd, didn't invite the suspicion that a speedboat might, and which was rugged enough to go offshore in foul weather, when nobody expected a transfer.

"He was smuggling?"

"No, Peter is a banker, always was, always will be. He worked the money end of things. Never handled drugs, except what he put up his own nose. But he was right in the middle of it all when that knock at the door came." Patti shook her head in self-loathing. "I was so stupid. I didn't have a clue what was going on until I got the call from his lawyer."

"How could you know?"

"I should have known."

"That's bullshit," I snapped. "Next you'll tell me Kevin and Natalie are to blame, too."

"Do they know? About their daddy?"

"No. I told them he was away on a very long business trip. Hell, it was true for a while."

"So, when they're saying good night to their daddy, they're not waving to Heaven."

"No, they're waving to him."

"What?" Liz asked, her eyes suddenly wide.

"His cell is on this side. He's got a little window."

"He's in prison over *there*? And he can see you? He can see us?"

"That's why he wanted us to move *No Name,* so he could see better. Better angle."

Liz looked suddenly pale and disoriented. "I don't believe this. He's watching us now?"

"He could be."

"But Patti," Liz struggled to understand, "why would you come here? Live under his prison window? I don't get it."

Patti covered her face with her hands. "You don't understand. I had nothing. No money. The Wisconsin house was in foreclosure. Peter had drained every account and I don't have any family to go to. We were living in the car, Liz. The babies were sick all the time. And then Peter said that one of his California friends, Samms, that's the guy who...." She touched her bruised cheek. "That Samms had managed to hide one asset from the Feds. The boat. It was in California and it could be mine. I could live on it free if I came out here. Just one condition."

"To moor it in Fish Harbor, so he could keep an eye on you."

"Wish Harbor," Patti said to herself in a small voice, in imitation of Natalie.

That was the thing that did it. Patti started to cry and before long it deepened into a real wail. I put my hand on her shoulder and was about to gather her in for a comforting hug. But it was into Liz's arms Patti fell for the solace she needed. That was okay with me. I understood that they were a lot closer than I was...than I was with just about anybody, really.

So I planted a kiss on Patti's forehead and left the two of them huddled on the afterdeck of *No Name*. I went home, to my canoe next door. I poured myself a stiff glass of whiskey and substituted it for toothpaste and brush. Five minutes later, I was lying in my berth with the porthole open for breeze when, dimly across the water, I heard Patti find her voice again:

"I'm just this stupid, mousy thing..."

"No, you're not," Liz protested.

"I follow him around, I have no life of my own. You're so free and...and Marion, too...free and not tied down. I'd give anything to be like you. I'm so tired of being me."

"Quiet now. Quiet...."

After that night, Patti Dell and Liz Thorsen were welded together. You hardly ever saw them apart except when Patti went to work. The four of them spent lots of time out in the channel aboard the sleek cruiser and less time aboard *No Name*. I missed Patti being a neighbor and the chatter from the kids, but I understood why she pulled away, after telling a big secret like that.

Patti asked me not to tell anyone else in Fish Harbor and I honored that request. The only thing I did was tell Tug that I had learned something pretty amazing. He said he didn't much care if he knew or not. That's what he said, but that didn't stop him from trying to guess. The old fart kept pestering me with wild theories and what-ifs, like this was a game of twenty questions.

"She's smuggling in Chinese at night."

"You saw the tail, didn't you? She *is* a mermaid."

The interesting thing was that Tug always supposed that the secret was about Liz. Typical of a man to assume that only someone drop-dead gorgeous could have a secret. At least, that's what I thought he thought. Pretty shallow of me, really, to underestimate Tug that way.

I was crossing the channel in my skiff a few days later and I saw Liz coming around the breakwater in her Zodiac. I flagged her down, she cut her engine, and we talked for a while, bobbing in the chop of intersecting wakes.

"How is she doing? I can't get two words out of her."

"She's okay. It's real embarrassing for her. She thinks everybody knows."

"I haven't told a soul."

"Me, neither. But you can see why."

"Why what?"

"Why she feels like everybody's watching her." She cast her eyes over at the prison. "He sits up there at the window and keeps an eye on everything."

"The husband?"

"And his prison friends and who knows who. She goes in to visit him and he asks about things. I mean, about us. He knows who you are, he knows who I am. He knows what we do every day. And if Kevin and Natalie miss one time saying good night, he throws a fit. It's really creepy. She hates going to visit him."

"But she still goes."

"Yes."

"Because she still sort of loves him."

"It's strange, isn't it?"

"Haven't you ever been in love, Liz?"

Liz fixed those snow-blue eyes on me. "Never like that," she pronounced.

"Is there anything I can do?"

"I've been trying to get her to, you know, take some kind of action to show that she can't live like this. What I think she wants to do is move."

"Move? Ashore?"

"No, move her boat. Like maybe back where it was before. So she's not living where he can always see her."

I couldn't retain the groan that escaped my lips. "Is that a lot of trouble?" Liz asked.

"It was a ton of trouble to get her the space next to me," I sighed. "Maybe it will be less trouble to move her back. When does she want to do it?"

"I'm not sure she's made up her mind yet. Give her some time."

"Okay. And what about that Samms guy? He hasn't been bothering her, has he?"

"No. But I gave her my cell phone. To call for help in case he does."

"Good idea."

Then came silence and we floated apart. With somebody else I might have asked how things were going, or a guy how they were hanging. But I didn't really know Liz, so we just continued to drift until I took a half stroke with my oars and she, in reply, pulled the cord on her outboard.

"Bye."

"See you."

Patti came to me about a week later, asking to make the move. It took another week of maneuvering and begging to return her to where she and *No Name* started out. She still hadn't done anything with that engine so it was another tow job to get her in the new slip. Her gratitude made it worth the effort, though. "Thank you, Marion," Patti said as she gave me a big hug. "I'm so lucky to have you for a friend."

"You've got a lot of friends."

I hadn't even mentioned her name but Patti smiled at the thought of Liz Thorsen. "She's just been wonderful. Do you know that 'Angel' show that used to be on TV?"

"No."

"The kids used to watch it."

"Liz is your angel, huh?"

"Does that sound stupid?"

What could I say, except: "She sure looks the part."

That was the summer of the El Nino when we had tons of rain, the ocean temperature shot up, and there was a three- or four-day period when there were actually albacore just outside the harbor. You don't usually see them north of San Diego, at least close on shore. It was a floating parking lot out there as every dentist and roofer and screenwriter with a skiff was trying his luck, but nobody had better luck than Danny. He went out every day for a week and filled everybody's icebox with filets. I made room in the ice cream freezer and the filets piled up in there, too. Anybody in Fish Harbor was free to come in and take some for dinner.

With all the boxes and freezers full, the boys decided they'd smoke the rest. Hanks used to do welding, so he and Alex and Harmon put together a smoker, mating together two old barbeque grills that had been rusting in back of the picnic area. Mr. Karandas brought home a bunch of mesquite and hickory wood from his restaurant and they had a slow smoky fire going by the time Danny returned, listing as always, with a really nice tuna.

Nobody in his right mind would want to miss this, so I made sure Patti knew and asked her to tell Liz. "The kids and me'll be there," she replied. She'd come out of her self-imposed shell more over the last week and seemed to be looking forward to dinner and beers with the rest of us. "But Liz won't come, I'm pretty sure."

"Why not?"

"She got a call. Actually, I got it, on the phone she loaned to me. The professor in charge of the research she's doing is coming sometime today, to check on the progress."

"He can join us."

"She says they'll be hours going over her findings and notes. It's really important. And she's a little nervous."

"Well, okay. Tell her good luck for me."

"If I see her. She hasn't even come out on deck since she got the news. Organizing it all, I guess."

"Yeah."

That's what she told me and that's what she told the guys, too, later, as we all lubed it up with beer and shooters, waiting for Danny's slabs of flaky, dry fish to cool down. Patti was enjoying herself more than I'd ever seen her. She saw that Liz and I had kept our mouths shut and now the pain of admitting her history was becoming part of the past. I even think she was flirting a little, with Hanks. I know he was having refreshed thoughts about her. I know the look.

It was just past dark and Danny was almost ready to dish it up when headlights swept across the picnic area and stopped, rudely lighting us all up like…well, like you know what.

"Hey," several voices cried at once, "who's making a movie?"

"Go be a fucking filmmaker somewheres else!"

The headlamps went out, revealing a black limousine in the parking lot where, I can assure you, none had ever parked before. A chauffeur in a suit walked around and opened the passenger's door. A man in his early sixties got out, dressed in real expensive "outdoor" clothing. His hair was silver and sleek.

He pulled a wicker basket from the back seat of the limo, the kind you buy at fancy liquor stores for business gifts at Christmas and such. I saw a couple of bottles sticking out of the cellophane as he walked down the ramp to the floating dock and waited. No more than thirty seconds later Liz rounded the corner in her Zodiac and came in for a landing. She knew we were all hanging out at the tables, just above the dock, but she never looked. The silver-haired guy got in the inflatable and Liz ferried him away to the blue cruiser without a saying word, to him or to us.

The headlights of the limo flared up again, then it backed out onto the street and disappeared.

It was like somebody threw a big canvas of quiet over the dinner. Danny served up the smoked albacore without saying a thing. Everybody chewed in silence.

"Well?" the big man finally asked, a little peeved.

"Yeah, great…Delicious…Great, Danny…."

"Looks like the professor game is picking up."

Leave it to Tug. I hate him sometimes. "What's that supposed to mean?" I shot back.

"There's nothing says a professor can't be rich," Patti spoke up, sort of out of nowhere. Everybody looked at her. "Maybe he invented something, like a computer chip."

"Like a new kind of dolphin vent," Tug suggested, but with obvious irony.

"Yeah, something like that."

The night went on, through second helpings of tuna and several more six-packs. The talk veered off the subject of the professor and returned to the usual stuff. But there was that subject, that question always hanging in the air. And I noticed one other thing: everyone was keeping a secret eye on the cruiser moored in the channel. The cabin lights in Liz's boat burned brightly and were reflected in a shimmering pathway across the water, sort of connecting Liz to land and to Patti. So it was an almost physical shock to Patti when, about ten-thirty, those lights went out.

Everybody waited a minute, a discreet sixty seconds. The Zodiac might appear, the limo return. But none of that happened. Danny said it first. "Spending the night, looks like."

"Yep."

"A very lucky professor."

"Must have invented something big."

"It's probably going to take several days," Alex added, his speech a little slurred from the tequila, "to get through all that 'research' she's been gathering."

"Bullshit," Hanks added.

"It's not bullshit," Patti said as loudly as she dared, not wanting to wake the kids sleeping on either side of her. "I helped her gather samples and take pictures. I told you about it, remember, Tug?"

"I remember what you said you did, Patti," Tug responded slowly. "But I've got to tell you, it didn't make much sense to me. California Fisheries *and* the Coast

Guard check the boats for dolphin release. EPA, Harbor, State, they're in here all the time, all over the harbor, taking samples of water. Who needs Liz Thorsen for that? Who needs pictures of fishing boats tied up for the night?"

"It's part of her grant. It's what she does."

I finally stepped in. "What she does is nobody's business but her own."

"That's right," Patti agreed. "You don't hear her making comments about what you do all day. Fishing. Scraping hulls. Collecting unemployment." She pointed out Danny, Alex, and Hanks in succession. Hanks' face tightened with suppressed anger. Her raised voice had awakened her kids. She picked them both up, a limp burden on each hip. "Come on, babies, time for bed."

"It's Veterans' benefits," Hanks shot back at her, "and I earned it."

Patti carried her kids down the ramp toward *No Name*.

"And I don't have to fuck some old guy to keep it!" Hanks shouted after Patti at the top of his tequila-filled lungs.

When I opened up around nine the next morning, the limo was back in the parking lot. The driver was leaning on the hood smoking a cigarette, so I walked over. Two grocery bags from Gelson's lay on the ground at his feet.

"Waiting for your boss?"

"Yeah, sort of. Waiting to deliver some stuff."

"You can leave it with me, if you want."

"No, I better wait."

"Where does he teach?"

"Teach?"

"Your boss? Isn't he a professor?"

"Mr. Knowles? He's a record producer."

"No research? Marine biology?"

"Hell, no. First time I've even seen him on that boat."

Then I heard Liz's outboard coming through the Marina. From the raised viewpoint of the parking lot I could see hatches opening all over. Everybody knew that sound. Everybody came out of his canoe to watch her drive in. She was sitting up straight in the Zodiac with her wet-suit top on, like the first day I'd seen her, except this time she was as stiff as a board, eyes straight ahead and lips pressed tightly together. Patti watched as the launch came skirting around the stern of *No Name*, saying nothing even though the boat was close enough to touch.

The driver lugged the heavy bags down to the dock and helped Liz stow them aboard. Then she returned to the cruiser without a word to any of us or a glance in our direction. It was hard to know what she was feeling. Was this pride or shame? Or did she just not care what anyone thought?

Patti stopped into the office on her way to her half day at the dry docks. "I saw you talking to that driver," she said, or rather she asked, for it was definitely a question. I didn't play games with her. I told her what he'd said. The look on her face broke my heart. She laid her teeth on her lower lip, biting to keep the disappointment down. "Tug was right," she said and walked out of the office.

It was good that Patti was at work that morning, because about eleven o'clock Liz brought the Zodiac back to the dock, this time with Knowles as passenger. Their parting was witnessed again by just about everyone in Fish Harbor. It was circumspect and formal, a handshake, a kiss on the cheek, but the undertow was obvious.

That was the last time I saw Liz Thorsen, at least close up. Everything more I learned from Patti Dell. 'Course I'm not sure Patti's telling the whole story and she may be smart not to.

Liz only stayed in Fish Harbor for another week after Knowles's visit. But it didn't seem to me that anything much had changed for her. She didn't come ashore but her routine on board the blue cruiser didn't seem to change at all. She still went out on her "research" trips in the kayak at night. She still took the Zodiac into Pedro for supplies. She dressed the same and looked the same. The way we looked at her changed but she just went on with her life.

According to Patti, that was the scary thing about it. I stopped by her canoe one night to see how she was doing. The kids were asleep and I think she was eager for somebody to talk to. A few hours after Liz's "professor" gathered up his empty champagne bottles and drove off in the limo, Patti borrowed Mr. K.'s skiff and rowed out to talk to Liz. Patti's voice wavered and cracked as she told me about the short visit.

"It was really strange, Marion. She would not talk to me about it."

"I can understand that."

"No, I mean she wouldn't admit anything. I told her about what everyone saw, and what Tug had said, about her 'research' just being an excuse to live on a nice boat and screw a rich old man instead of working for a living."

"Patti, Tug never said that!"

"Oh, that's what he meant and you know it. That's what they all think. And…and it's the truth."

I didn't contradict her. She was right about me, I did think that.

"But she just kept going on, ignoring reality, saying how her work is important and that the silver haired guy is just a good friend helping her with the final report. 'Which took all night?' I asked her. 'And six bottles of wine?'"

"Patti, it could be that this is none of your business."

"Of course it's none of my business. Liz can sleep with whoever she wants. It's just...the lie of it all."

"It's not the first time somebody's lied to you, is it?"

"No, but..."

"But what, honey?"

"Why do I always fall for it? All the time Peter was in California, there I was sitting at home, good little trusting wife. And now here comes Liz. I trusted her. And she was a real help to me, Marion, after I told you guys about everything. I mean a real help. She listened to me cry and listened to me be pissed off. She *made* me move the boat back, to show Peter I wasn't going to do what he said anymore. She went with me to prison and held my hand right up to the gate. You know what I was doing? I was trading Peter for her."

"You can't compare the two of them. I don't think Liz is lying to you, as much as she's lying to herself."

Patti absorbed that idea for a moment. "Maybe so," she said finally. "Who can look at their life in the mirror and call it like it is?"

"Nobody I know."

"Anyway, she'll be gone soon. Moving on to the next big thing. Lots of other yachts and mansions to house-sit. I don't think I'll see her again."

"It's hard when angels fall, huh?"

"Yeah."

That was why the Fourth of July was such a surprise. I didn't expect that Patti and Liz would be seeing each other after that. I sure didn't expect that they'd be celebrating the holiday together.

Every year since they hauled the Queen into dry dock, the City of Long Beach has been shooting off its annual fireworks from a barge anchored just astern of the old liner. It's quite a zoo out there, with maybe three hundred boats of all sizes anchored and floating around just at sundown. Every Harbor Patrol and County Lifeguard and Coast Guard vessel in the harbor is there to try and maintain order. It's fun, right up to the moment just after the fireworks, when three hundred boats all want to get to the slip or the launch ramp at once, in the dark.

Some years we go, some not. Danny decided he'd motor over this year, so Hanks and me went along. Tug was working. As we left Fish Harbor, I noticed that Patti's canoe was dark and Liz's blue cruiser was off on one of its "missions."

We dropped the hook in a likely spot and popped some tops and waited. I took Danny's binoculars and started looking around. See and be seen was part of the fun out there. I looked it over for maybe forty minutes as it got darker. With so many boats in the dying light, it was just by chance that I happened to see her. The blue cruiser, I mean, floating at the edge of the anchorage area. Danny's glasses were good: There was no mistaking Liz at the flying bridge and Patti and her kids on the bow, getting ready for the show. As I watched them for some clue about how they were getting along, Samms came out of the cabin and climbed up to join Liz.

"What the fuck," I said without thinking.

"What?"

"Look over here." I pointed Danny toward the cruiser and handed him the glasses.

"You see Liz?"

"Yeah. But isn't that…?"

"Yeah, that's that guy."

"What's going on?"

"I don't know." I went below to Danny's VHF and auto-tuned it to Channel Sixteen. But you can imagine: three hundred boats and everybody wanting to talk to his neighbor. I couldn't get a piece of clear air to save my life and there was no way to declare an emergency, really, legitimately.

"I don't like it."

"What do you want to do?"

"Go over there."

But that was easier said than done. Everybody was anchored in pretty tight together and Danny's hook wouldn't break free of the mud on the first try. At that moment, of course, they decided to start the fireworks, adding to our confusion and the number of skippers we were pissing off by trying to leave in the middle of the show. I let the guys wrestle with the anchor as I kept my eyes glued to the cruiser. It would be easy to lose sight of them if I didn't. Were they watching us back? It sure seemed like it, because as soon as we showed signs of picking up anchor, Patti and her kids disappeared below and the cruiser turned one-eighty and headed for the breakwater. It picked up speed quickly and steered straight for the entrance.

"Hey, just forget it," I told the guys. "She's running out to sea and we'd never catch her in this."

"Why's she heading out?"

"I don't know."

That's what I said, but I knew what I knew. Samms was a smuggler, aboard a speedy boat, on a night when every law enforcement vessel was busy playing traffic cop. With the kids aboard as leverage. It worried the shit out of me. I barely looked up at the Chinese fire in the sky over my head.

The show was over in half an hour. Danny worked his way through the mob scene and got us back to Fish Harbor not long after that. I thought about trying to raise Liz on the VHF again, but I didn't know if that would help or cause more jeopardy for them. I stayed up, pacing the office floor.

They idled back into Fish Harbor about eleven that night, after the place had mostly gone to bed. This time, for the first time, Liz brought the blue cruiser into the dock. She didn't even bother to tie up, just brought the boat alongside while Patti, Kevin, and Natalie jumped off. There was no gesture of farewell between them, but Liz did see me in the office and waved once. I waved back. Then she put the cruiser in gear and pulled away. She steered it past the buoy where she usually tied up and disappeared around the groin into the outer harbor. That was the last I saw of Liz Thorsen.

I gave Patti a few minutes to settle her kids in. When the forward cabin lights went out, I walked down to talk to her. We sat in the cockpit of *No Name* passing a pint bottle of brandy between us and I told her what I had seen.

She nodded, then shook her head angrily. "That son of a bitch!"

"Samms?"

"No, my son of a bitch husband. Samms didn't know anything about Liz. Peter told him. Peter's been watching us."

"I don't understand."

"Samms showed up here this afternoon. He didn't even bother to ask about my boat this time, he just *told* me: My friend Liz was taking us all for a ride. I said I wouldn't call her. But...you know...he made threats. He said things would happen to Peter in prison if...if I didn't do what he said."

"Bullshit."

"Yeah, probably, but the kids were there, too. He didn't have to say it; I knew he'd hurt them if he didn't get what he wanted. He belted me before. So…"

"She came?"

Patti looked out at the water of the channel, at the point where Liz and the cruiser had disappeared. "You know, Marion, she wasn't an angel, but she was there for us. She didn't hesitate a minute. She took us where Samms wanted to go. But she didn't take any shit from him. Anytime that asshole reminded us of what he could do, she told him, just flat and cold, that she'd pay him back for what he did. My family…were people she loved, that's what she said. I tell you, he was afraid of her."

"Good."

"Yeah, good. Yeah, real good. I mean, I felt like…well, there were the two of us, two women who'd allowed men to fuck with us…or maybe *invited* men to fuck with us… but we weren't going to do it anymore. Samms was it. Samms was the last."

Patti stopped talking but I had the feeling that words were still going through her head. A speech to herself. Finally I had to ask: "So what happened?"

"It got rough out in the ocean. I put the kids below and told them to stay there."

"What happened…with Samms?"

"We, uh…we met up with this boat, out there a few miles."

"And they gave you drugs?"

"No, no…we…Samms went over to them."

"He transferred to the other boat?"

"Yeah."

"At sea? That must have been fun."

"What do you mean?"

"I mean dangerous."

"Yeah, I guess so."

A few moments later she said: "Liz isn't coming back."

"That's too bad."

"It's good for her. It's time she went on to something else. It's time for me, too."

"You're leaving, Patti?"

She nodded. "It's been good living here. This was a place I had to come to, I know that. But if I stay here, I'll always be, you know, in the shadow of that place. I'll always be his wife and there will always be another Samms or somebody. I have to make a break now. I couldn't before but I can now."

We did see Liz Thorsen again actually, about a year later.

Patti and the kids moved out immediately after the Fourth of July. She sold *No Name* and put the money down in deposit on an apartment in Pedro. Mr. K. took her on full time as a waitress. I had seen her once since she moved, Thanksgiving dinner at the restaurant. She looked fine. Kevin was six and starting first grade and Natalie was in Kindergarten.

Then one day the next spring, Mr. K. came to work and told Patti that he had seen Liz Thorsen in a movie. It was IMAX, that big-screen deal at the Science Museum downtown. He'd been there with some out-of-town relatives and seen a movie called "Great Circle Route." It was about ocean sailboat racing and he was positive that Liz Thorsen was a member of the crew that had been filmed racing across the Pacific.

Two weeks later Tug and I picked up Patti and her kids and drove up the freeway to Exposition Park. Those kids were still a pair of real sweeties, curious and talkative but polite and respectful. Patti was a champ in the mom department.

We sat in the third row as that screen stretched far below and above us. The action of the ocean was so convincing that some people around us actually got sick. Then, about ten minutes in, the story focused on one racing boat and how her crew trained. The kids let out a cry as we saw Liz, huge and lifelike, working lines on the foredeck. Her blonde hair was cut boy-close but she was still a real stunner. Another shot confirmed that it was her: she was sitting around the galley table, off watch with other crew members, wearing a hooded sweatshirt which read "Fish Harbor" in bright letters across the front. I had sold her that top.

"Fish Harbor," Natalie cried out. Damned if that child couldn't read. At five.

I tried to sneak a look at Patti. It was hard because she was sitting right next to me but I'm pretty sure she was enjoying herself. I remembered when Patti was jealous of Liz and her freedom. But like I told Tug that one time, envy in women can be poison but it can also be sweet and give birth to good will if it comes out of the right kind of friendship.

All of a sudden Patti stiffened. I looked back up at the screen. The narrator had been talking about training for emergencies at sea, "…including the most feared emergency of all: Man Overboard." On deck, the sailboat crew was about to run a recovery drill. Liz stood on the foredeck next to a man-sized target dummy. On command she put her shoulder to the dummy and jolted it sharply over the gunwale and into the sea.

Patti looked away from the screen for a moment, but then she turned and met my gaze. Her mouth was curled up in the strangest, crooked, half cruel smile. It was like she had given me a riddle and was enjoying my floundering to solve it. Except I'm pretty sure I did solve it. I just never said the answer and I never will.

Tug drove me home and he didn't say much. I know how he feels about sailboat racing, that it's a stupid game for overgrown rich kids, so I didn't expect him to like the movie. As we came down off the bridge and into the square sides of Fish Harbor, he finally spoke: "I guess I just don't get it."

"Get what, baby?"

"Patti and Liz, turning out to be friends. What the hell did they have in common?"

He was right. He doesn't get it.

"THE ANNUAL MEETIING OF THE AMERICAN SOCIETY OF LONE FISHERMEN WHO HAVE FOUND DEAD BODIES"

A one-man expedition

By

T.S. Cook

This play was first performed at a

benefit gala on December 6, 2011

at Theatre/Theater in Los Angeles.

Starring: Paul Messinger

Directed by: TS Cook

Set and stagecraft design by Chris Cook

THE ANNUAL MEETING
OF THE AMERICAN SOCIETY
OF LONE FISHERMEN
WHO HAVE FOUND DEAD BODIES

(Lights up on the hull of a fishing skiff, maybe 19 feet long. It is equipped with a steering station—wheel, compass, GPS, marine radio with mic. There is a stern-mounted rod holder, a boat hook, and a length of coiled line. A lone Angler is at the wheel, steering. He wears a thin self-inflating life vest and a sun hat tied down. Wind blows in his face and an outboard motor thrums behind him.)

(The Angler divides his attention between steering the boat and looking at the GPS. Now he sees something he likes and brings the boat to a stop, killing the motor.)

ANGLER

The proverbial 'likely spot.'

(He strips off the life vest and pulls a rod from a holder. Opening his tackle box, he selects a hook and begins tying it to the line. He stops once and looks up, looks around at the sea, and smiles.)

ANGLER

Yeah, see, this is what I'm talking about!
Pure, simple, alone-itude. Can't see the
mainland, can't see the islands. Can't see
shit. Can't hear shit. No hat-turned-back-
ward fool who thinks he's Dr. Dre pulled
up next to you. Nothing, blissful nothing
and nobody. I love being out here. On land,
back there...

> (Checks the compass.)

ANGLER

Well, actually, there...I'm never alone. I
live in the middle of one of the world's
biggest cities. And when I go home and shut
the door, my wife is there. I love my wife
but she is, in fact, always there. We both
live at home, we're both writers so we both
work at home, we sleep there, we eat the
same thing, read the same thing, it never
ends. But my wife, God love her, has one
quality that makes it all worth it: She
hates fishing. And then there's people I
meet who say..."Oooo, I love the sea. Can
you take me out sometime?" No. If I take
you fishing, then I'm not fishing, I'm a fishing guide.

> (He lowers his rig over the
> side.)

ANGLER

All right. Ringing the dinner bell...See, what I'm doing here? This is what I come out here to do. Fish. Not to socialize, not to catch up on all the gossip. Fish. Well, I also drink...

    (Angler pulls a pint bottle
    from his pocket and takes a
    swig.)

ANGLER

Let me put it this way: did you hear the story about the old Cajun and the fish and game girl. So, there's this brand new cute college-grad fish and game officer working the docks on the Bayou Anglais. Talking to the guys, getting to know the boats. And she notices that there's this one old guy, Marcel, who always comes home with a boat-load of fish. Even when everybody else gets skunked, he's always at the dock, weighing in. So she turns on the charm and casually says, "Gee, I'd sure like to know what your secret is." He says, "Shore, girly, I'll take you out." So the next day they're back heading upriver and off the channel back to a deep hole he knows. Marcel cuts the outboard and smiles and says, "Here's my secret." He reaches into his tackle box and takes out a ten-ounce lead sinker lashed to a stick of dynamite, lights it and throws it overboard. That black water goes THOMMMP! And a moment later hundreds of stunned fish come floating to the surface. Old Marcel starts slowly scooping them in with his net. The fish and game girl is fucking outraged. "What? You can't do that! That's against every game law...That's a thousand dollar fine...I'm placing you under arrest..." And as she is blustering on, old Marcel reaches in and comes up with another stick of dynamite. He lights it and tosses it to her and says: "You gonna bitch, or fish?"

> (Laughs, another swig.)

ANGLER

"You gonna bitch or fish?" That pretty much sums up my philosophy about...pretty much everything. So, thank you, you've been a great audience, good night...Naw, stick around. Besides...

> (gestures to the sea, a
> wicked smile.)

Where you gonna go?

> (He turns on the Very High
> Frequency marine radio and
> adjusts the squelch. It
> crackles a few times.)

ANGLER

Always keep this on out here. You never know. Ah, I drank a ton of coffee.

> (He heaves himself up onto
> the upstage gunwale and un-

zips. The sound of a urine
stream hitting the ocean
surface.)

ANGLER

Ahhhh....All the ocean for my urinal. All
the earth my ashtray. Hey, here's one for
you. Statistic. Did you know the one thing
something like 65% of all male drowning
victims have in common?

> (He turns to face down-
> stage. He has left his fly
> open. He points to it.)

ANGLER

You know: Whitey's out of jail. Security
breach at Los Pantalones. Because when the
urge to whiz becomes unbearable, and we
lean out so we don't dribble the lemonade
on our friend's freshly waxed hull, in the
ecstasy of release we sometimes forget the
first rule of safe boating: one hand for the
boat, one hand for the choat.

> (He zips up. Checks the set
> of the reel.)

ANGLER

> (to the fish)

Come on. I know you're down there and I
know you're hungry...I've often wondered

what my first thought would be, if I fell overboard like that. Would it be..."Oh my God, I'm overboard in six hundred feet of the Pacific, with my life hanging on what I do next." Or would it be: "Fuck, I'm swimming in my own piss!" I think it would be the piss. Like most things, like growing old: First the disgust, then the horror.

(Indicates the life vest.)

ANGLER

I wear the vest when I'm underway. I've never fallen overboard, knock on fiberglass. But, shit, it can happen. You can fall overboard any time. It happened right here to a friend of mine. Calm day, flat sea. George was my bartender. Great guy, with a great pour, half of the time for free. Every time I'd come in the bar he'd shout out "Hey, Big Fella." Where everybody knows your name, right? Six-foot-five black man with a handshake that would crush a brick. Vietnam vet but never a hard word for a draft dodger like me. Anyway, George was feeling kind of blue one night 'cause he'd been popped for DUI the week before. He told us all the story and it did sound like a bogus bust. But you know, with Mothers Against God-damn Everything, you're guilty as soon as you roll the window down. George was going to fight the charges, a resolve we bar patrons saluted with...raised cocktails. So I broke my policy and said, "Let's go fishing," to raise his spirits, and a few days later we did. Out to the nine-mile kelp for rock cod. Hooked into a few right away, then the bite settled down. George was having a good time, crying "Fuck!" to the sky, and bitching about the bust and his three-thousand-dollar lawyer. So I started telling him my favorite lawyer joke. And while I was...Oh, wait, you want to hear it? So, see, this guy gets arrested for fucking a goat. And he goes to his buddy the lawyer for advice. And his buddy says: "Look, I can't help you, I'm not a criminal lawyer. But here's my advice to you: There's basically two ways to go. You can hire a lawyer who is really sharp at the rules of evidence and knows how to argue before a judge. Or you can go with the lawyer who is really good at picking a jury. Both have their advantages, but if it was me, and I was looking at a jury trial on these charges, I'd go with the jury picker." So the guy takes the advice and he hires the local lawyer who is good at picking twelve men and true. So, first day of evidence, the state's star witness is old Mrs. Smith. the guy's neighbor: "What did you see, Mrs. Smith?" "I saw the defendant come out of his house into the back yard where he kept the goat tied up. And then....then he pulled down his pants and had sex with that animal." "I see, and then what happened?" "Well, then he slowly walked around to the front of the goat and the goat...licked him clean." One juror turns to the next and says: "A good goat'll do that."

(Angler cracks up at his
own story.)

ANGLER

I love that joke. Even lawyers love that
joke. So, I tell the punch line and I
don't hear any laughter, so I look around
and...no George! Gone. Vanished. I mean,
where does a six-foot-five black man go on a
nineteen foot boat made out of white fiberglass? Only one place—overboard. So I look
down and sure enough there's two Godzilla
hands holding on. I didn't hear a splash.
I didn't hear a shout for help. But there's
George, looking up at me, as surprised as
I've ever seen anyone be. So now we have a
physics problem. I mean...

(Demonstrates the positions.)

ANGLER

Here's George and here's the surface of
the water and here's the handholds. No
place to put your feet, to push yourself
up. So, unless you've been cashing pay-
checks from Cirque de Soleil for the last
six years, you're fucked. I reach down
to try and help him but there's nothing
to hold onto. Except his t-shirt, which
I promptly rip right off his back trying.
But not to worry. Because there is always
the "sailors' solution to everything." Do

you know what is the "sailors' solution to everything?"

(Picks up the coil of line.)

ANGLER

Line. You gotta love line. I mean—look at it. Archimedes said, "Give me a lever and I can move the world." Right, there's a land lubber's perspective for you. What fucking good is a lever out here? Line, my friends.

(As he starts to rig a come-along.)

ANGLER

You know the difference between a Republican and a Democrat. If a man is drowning a hundred feet off shore, a Republican will throw him sixty feet of line and tell him to swim the rest of the way, because it will build character. A Democrat will throw the man two hundred feet of line, and then walk away. Oh, right, drowning, George.

(Demonstrating, he throws a fast bowline loop for George's chest.)

ANGLER

In the end I actually had to winch him aboard. He was chilled to the bone so that was the end of fishing that day. He wrapped up in the thermal blanket and I ran in for shore. But...we weren't done yet. We were coming in to the dock. George was up in the bow. "Just sit tight," I told him. I put her nose in, looked around to make sure the stern was cocked right. I turn back. No George. Gone. Again. Where does a six-foot-five black man wrapped in a silver blanket go? Overboard. Again. Only this time, it's no joke. This time he's down between the dock and the boat, and the current is pushing the hull in towards him. This is how skulls get crushed. I convince him to let go of the boat and grab the dock. And about this time some Baywatch guys come running. They saw what happened and they were the ones who pulled him out. So, all in all, quite a day. After that, when I'd walk into the bar and George'd say "Hey, Big Guy," I'd always answer...

(Comic gay tone)

ANGLER

"Hey, Sailor."

(The reel sings to life, a
fish running with the bait.)

ANGLER

Oh! Hello! That's what I'm taking about!

> (He carefully eases the rod
> out of its holder and sets
> the hook. The rod bends
> over steeply and the drag
> begins to unspool.)

ANGLER

Yes! Git on there! Fish on! Okay, okay, you take as much line as you want. Look at this guy go.

> (The fish stops taking line
> and the angler begins to
> pump his equipment.)

ANGLER

Okay, my turn now...Come on up...Man, is there anything to compare with having a fish on the line? The Buddhists talk about being centered and being in the moment. Here and now, they say, here and now. Well, fucking here and now! I think you catch a fish as much by willpower as by mechanical advantage...Okay, ready to come up? Come on...You can tell different fish from their bite and the way they play the line. Halibut feel like you hooked into an old tire until they get sight of the boat, then they go as nuts as a raped ape. Barracuda just bite and keep going, like the torpedos they are. This is a rock fish. Fighting like hell down in the kelp but slowly los-

ing the will as the contest drags on. Like
the Dodgers in post season.

> (The fish action is smaller
> and more localized now.
> Never taking his eyes off
> the line, he puts his hand
> overboard.)

ANGLER

Okay. Color! Coming up. Come on....And
Gotcha!

> (He grabs a large copper-
> colored fish which squirms
> mightily.)

ANGLER

All right! Yes! Chucklehead.

> (He holds his prize up.)

ANGLER

How about that? Look at this guy. Look at
the color of him. All copper red here and
gold along the spine. Look into that eye,
my friends, and what do you see? Man, this
is why I fish, this moment. To pull this
creature out of a place so alien and look
him in the eye. Feel that deep cold slime
he lives in, look at his fins and hackles
all up and spiny and pissed off. Chucklehead. No, no, that's not a putdown, just

a nickname. Proper name would be...*Scorpaenidae sebastes*, I think. Pacific Copper Rockfish. Also called: Chucklehead. Also called: Never Die. That's one of the unique things about this fish. They are famous for staying alive out of the water. This guy will still be kicking in the trunk on the ride home.

> (He puts the Never Die in
> a fish locker, then stops,
> looks at house.)

ANGLER

Oh, okay, I can hear it coming. We're going to have the argument now. "You mean you are going to kill that beautiful fish and eat it?" Yes, I am. "You mean, with everything that's available to you as a modern urban man, you are going to revert to killing wild animals for meat?" Yes, I am. "Well, you say all those poetic things about the fish and his hidden ecology but really you're just a caveman!" Yes, I am. But allow the "Caveman" to say a few words in his defense. First off, Caveman obey all Fish and Game laws. Caveman buy fishing license in the first week of January every year and Caveman donate hundreds of dollars to green causes, ocean related or not. Every year, if I am lucky, I will keep and eat one fish only of any legal species I catch. I keep only one fish per trip. All other fish go back in. If Caveman catch another dozen fish today, all of them go back in. Caveman is basically a catch-and-release fisherman, just like all you vegetarians out there are...basically vegetarians. Besides, if you want to insult me, calling me a caveman won't work because I am a caveman. We are all cavemen, or women, it's just that I acknowledge my caveman-hood. Consider: Fishing is the last large-scale activity done by modern man that was also done by our prehistoric ancestors. Fish we catch, everything else we manufacture. Many of you who are distressed by my plan to make chucklehead chowder would eagerly scarf down the Wolfgang Puck-roasted breast of a bird whose last months of life were spent in horrendous industrial conditions, even if it says "free range" on the menu. What's more free-range than the bottom of the sea? Caveman say: Fishing is authentic. Caveman say: Fishing connects us to the past. But only if you eat the fish.

(The Never Die thumps loudly
in the fish locker.)

ANGLER

(to Never Die)

I'm glad you agree. So, all right: first fish! First, biggest, most. That's the fisherman's wager. It's the classic bet on fishing trips. Everybody puts in fifteen bucks. Whoever catches the first fish collects five

from everyone. Whoever catches the biggest
fish collects the same. And the man with the
most fish at the end of the day collects
the rest. It sounds simple and it's moron
easy to administer, but the way it plays
out is pretty interesting. For example,
you always want to catch that first fish. A:
because you have already made your money
back. And B: because fish react excitedly
to the first food in the water, then get
rapidly fickle...

    (Never Die thumps.)

              ANGLER

Sorry, it's true...and they often don't
bite again for the rest of the day. Which
means first fish often collects it all. Most
fish is also desirable, because if you have
the most it is very likely that you also
have the first and biggest. But biggest,
it's the one everybody wants to win because...well, come on...because this is
America. Size matters, right? You never
see "first fish" over the mantelpiece.

    (Slides the re-baited line
    into the water and lets it
    sink to the bottom.)

              ANGLER

I can immodestly say that I have won in all
categories in my fish-stinking life. I won
120 bucks on a rock cod trip out of Morro

Bay. And I've been robbed, too. Down in Mexico on a big long-distance boat, three days fishing for tuna. Twenty-five anglers aboard and a fifty buck buy-in meant a $1250 winner-take-all prize for biggest fish. And we got into them, too. We hit a bait ball that was turning out hundred-pound fish. My bait got struck. I had a monster on. Rod bent over double, line so tight you could pluck a high E. Twenty minutes I fought this thing—I thought my arms were gonna pull out of my shoulders. I finally muscle him up next to the hull. I call out for the deckhand. "Big boy," the kid says as he gets ready with the gaff. We're all set to land him. And then, from behind, a flash in the water and when the deckhand gets my fish up on deck...it's just a head. Everything from the gills aft, gone. Just like that. I didn't even feel a tug on the line when that shark hit. And, of course, at the end of the trip, I had the biggest *head* of a fish but somebody else went home with the twelve-fifty. (Never Die thumps.)

ANGLER

Oh, find that amusing, do you?

(Never Die thumps.)

ANGLER

Chowder.

> (The VHF crackles. Did he
> hear something? Decides he
> didn't.)

ANGLER

First, biggest, most. Like I said, as the
day unravels, the way you view the bet
changes. Just like the years unravel and
the bet changes. Who gets there first? Who
sells the first big screenplay? Who makes
partner or gets on staff...first? I can only
talk about men but I know this if I know
anything—this is the way we compete. And
for young men this is the race of their
lives. This is all that matters, when
you're twenty-something. 'I got started
before you did.' 'I have more talent and
so they saw it earlier.' 'I'm so happy that
they *now also finally* see that you have
talent'...But then the sun gets higher in
the sky and the bet changes. Who cares who
got there first? 'I made it biggest.' 'My
biggest movie was way bigger than yours.'
'Your biggest was a shark-bit head compared
to mine.' Biggest fish, biggest house, biggest second house. And then the sun starts
to go down and we count up the fish. Who's
got the most at the end of the day? You
may have caught a whopper at 10 AM...or at
thirty-one...but who remembers the thrill
of that now? Not even you. What's the sum
total of the...trip? It begins to matter

less how well others did. Did you catch
everything that you needed?

> (He adjust the line, shaking
> his head.)

ANGLER

Listen, don't pay me any mind. It's really silly, and absurdly reductive, to sug-
gest that men's lives can be modeled on
an activity that requires more bait than
brains. Still, I wonder if maybe a fourth
bet could be added. Five bucks from everybody in the pool to the fisherman who most
intensively appreciates spiritual interac-
tion with the fish.

> (The Never Die thumps.)

ANGLER

No, probably not. Not while we cavemen
still wander the earth.

> (The angler looks pensively
> out over the surface of the
> sea for a few beats. The
> VHF crackles with a mes-
> sage. It is extremely gar-
> bled but it sounds like a
> voice and the first three
> words could be "Mayday.")

ANGLER

What the fuck...

> (He fiddles with the squelch
> and volume. The message
> comes again, still incom-
> prehensible. He lifts the
> mic to his lips, thinks
> about it for a moment, then
> broadcasts.)

ANGLER

Vessel broadcasting on channel 16, are you
issuing a Mayday?

> (No reply.)

ANGLER

Vessel broadcasting on channel 16, this is
the fishing skiff Uncle Jack. Are you de-
claring an emergency? Over.

> (No reply.)

ANGLER

I guess it's nothing. Could be...A lot of
times it's kids, fooling around. They think
it's a toy. Serious fine from the Feds,
though, if you get caught. 1500 clams. I
never fuck around with an open mic, not out
here. But I mean, I'm no different from any
other joker. You see an unguarded bullhorn
and what do you do? "Paging Jesse Helms.
Senator Jesse Helms, please pick up the

whites-only courtesy telephone." Or the classic, just simply: "People of Earth!" You'd be surprised how many heads look up. 'Cause they all know, someday....

(Never Die thumps.)

That's right...Ah, wait, speaking of gags...

(He rummages around in his tackle box until he finds what he wants. He laughs and pulls out a sandwich baggie laden with some heavy round objects.)

ANGLER

Ha...Look. I thought these were still in here. Oh, man—does this bring back memories. A million years ago, when I had friends. Johnny and Birdman and me. And Jay sometimes. We terrorized the trout of the Sierras for a solid decade. And these...

(He is doubled over in laughter.)

ANGLER

So let me tell you what these are. I had them made. Johnny had a kid in junior high, in metal shop, and his kid made them for us. They're just lumps of lead that the kid melted together with some metallic yellow

dye. I'd stick them in my tackle box whenever we were taking some new guy with us
fishing. Somebody's brother or co-worker.
We'd drive up into the Sierras and then
hike a mile or so in and wet a line. And
after we'd been fishing for an hour or so,
if the bite was off, ever so casually I'd
reach into my backpack and take out...
the pan. And I'd start panning. For gold.
'Cause this river, you know, those old
49ers took tons of gold out of this place.
I'd swish the water and poke through the
sand. And the new guy was always fascinated by this. So sure, I'd show him how
to do it. Scoop out some likely sand from
the downstream side of a boulder. Circle
the water around just so, try and tickle
some color out of her. And before long, he
was on his hands and knees, rod up on the
bank, fishing flushed right out of his mind
by gold fever. And then, after a while...
we had this routine down cold...one of the
other guys would distract him and when he
wasn't looking, I'd drop one of these into
the pan.

(Overlapping different voices)

ANGLER

"Oh, fuck, man, what is that?!" "Did you
pan that?" "That is one big honking nugget,
man." "Go on, bite it." "That is fucking
solid gold, man!" "Gotta be three ounces."
"Fucking guy—we take him fishing once and

he makes a thousand dollars!" So after a bunch of back slapping and beer toasts, we pack up and head down to the jeep. And he's trying to be so cool and all, but every fifteen minutes he's digging the nugget out of his pocket and sneaking a look at it, you know. So we get back to the Jeep and we're driving into town. And I'm sitting shotgun and I say: "Hey, lemme see that stone again." So he's all smiles as he pulls it out and hands it to me. And I look it over, real jeweler and all, and then I just...toss it out the window! Birdman's got his camera ready and 'click!'....Hah! I got a collection of these nugget-out-the-window shots at home. And let me tell you: Fuck a bunch of slasher movies. You want to see real horror on the human face? I can show it to you.

(He simulates a few horrified expressions.)

ANGLER

It's funny, you know. You lose something in a moment and it's a shock. Your blood pressure goes through the roof. Particularly if you really didn't earn it to begin with. If it fell into your lap and then you lose it, that makes you crazy. If it happens gradually, that's different. If, say, you work at a job for thirty years and you never get that big raise, even though you earned it. If you see the way you live

going slowly down and down. If the jobs
don't come. Or the jobs go overseas. Now,
if the price of gas goes up fifteen cents
in a week, we're ready to burn down the
fucking White House. How dare you toss my
hydrocarbon nugget out the car window? But
if they slowly, deliberately, bit-by-bit
fuck the middle class, well, the middle
class just keeps fishing...And you know,
it's the same with friends. If we lose them
fast, like we lost Jay, it hurts. We cry.
But if we just sort of stop calling each
other, if it's too much trouble anymore to
pack up the Jeep, if we think, fuck, I've
heard that guy's stories a million times
already, then, you know what happens? You
wind up fishing alone.

> (He weighs the nuggets in
> his hand, then tosses a hand-
> ful overboard. He screams
> in mock horror and loss.
> Then, amusement, mixed with
> real loss...)

ANGLER

I got to call those guys.

> (He fishes in silence for
> a few beats. He coils the
> line out of habit.)

ANGLER

(with affection)

Line...It can save your life, it can make your life.

(The Never Die thumps.)

ANGLER

You don't believe me? True story: March 17, 1956. A nor'easter storm drives a huge Italian freighter, the *Etrusco*, onto the rocks south of Boston. Italian crew abandons ship. One local guy is sitting on his porch watching the whole thing.

(The reel clicks a few times promisingly. He watches it.)

ANGLER

He takes a length of line, not even as heavy as this, gets in his dory and rows out to the ship, where there's a chain hanging from the bow. He ties his line to the chain, rows back, ties the other end to his porch railing and shouts out: "Salvage!"

(More clicking. Never Die thumps. He moves toward the rod.)

ANGLER

And do you know what? The International Maritime Court awarded him possession of that ship. Line, my friends. The Italians had to pay him millions to get their freighter back. And today, that local man is John Kerry, US Senator from the State of Massachusetts.

> (mischievous beat)

No, he's not! But the rest of it's perfectly true.

> (The reel sings out—another fish on. Angler springs into action.)

                    ANGLER

Hello!

> (The fight is on again. The fish takes line; he reels it in. Back and forth along the upstage side of the boat they dance. Never Die thumping all along. Finally the Angler scoops in his prize—a red snapper.)

                    ANGLER

All right! Red Snapper.

> (As he pops out the hook...)

                    ANGLER

Dee-licious is the Red Snapper. But remember my promise to all you vegetarians. One fish per trip, so this guy goes back in. And the ling isn't like old Never Die there. You've got to get him back in the water fast. So what you want to do is keep his mouth open and pass him back and forth in the water....

> (He kneels over so the fish
> is out of sight overboard
> and moves him back and
> forth.)

ANGLER

Like this...Come on...And gone! Straight to the bottom. He's there already.

> (He stands, faces house, a
> hand over his heart.)

ANGLER

Caveman keep his word.

> (The VHF comes to life, a
> clear, high-powered trans-
> mission.)

LAND STATION

Securite. Securite. Securite. This is Coast Guard Station Long Beach with a notice to mariners. Stand by.

(Angler fiddles with radio
controls.)

LAND STATION

Securite. Securite. Securite. Coast Guard
Station Long Beach has monitored a possible
distress call off the Southern California
Coast, Point Dume to the San Clemente Island Two low-power transmissions occurred
at 0858 and 0900. Vessels in the area are
requested to keep lookout and render assistance. Coast Guard clear.

(The Angler sweeps the ho-
rizon with his binoculars.
He shakes his head.)

ANGLER

Nothing. But I think we're...

(checks the GPS)

Right. Dad's final resting place, just over
there. Three hundred yards, bearing 165. I
go out there every now and then. Just to
visit. I don't fish on the spot where we
buried Dad. When it comes my turn, though,
I won't mind. My plan is, well, there's
this company that takes your ashes and
mixes them into a big rough concrete ball,
all full of holes and fissures, and then
they dump you into the sea. As a home for
fish and such. So there you are: rascal one

moment, reef the next. The ultimate "give something back."

(Leaves the GPS station,
takes a seat. Ruminates a
beat.)

ANGLER

Burials...You know I was talking about George before, how he never thought badly of me even though I dodged the draft. I remember that first summer after college, my first trip to Europe, the first of many moves to fake out the Draft Board. I managed to get on an archeological expedition to, well, what was then called Yugoslavia. Which carried with it a very exotic scientific deferment. I mean, to be honest, the draft dodge is why I went, but it turned out there was a lot more to it. There was this one thing that happened...We were digging an exploratory trench out from the main site in an attempt to find the necropolis, the Roman graveyard. We had already found the corner of a Roman period house and inside there were some very exciting things, including a beautiful purple glass goblet, in fragments of course. But it was bones we were after, to be part of a large scale study of Roman remains for traces of lead and other elements. So there was a lot of excitement when the trench hit a burial. He was a man, about thirty, and intact. We spent all of that day on our hands and knees with our trowels and brushes and dental tools, cleaning away the dirt and taking pictures. It was getting close to quitting time when we looked up from the trench and saw three old women looking down. We knew who they were. They lived in a house nearby, just the three of them, "the old crones" we called them. They kept the expedition's tools locked in their barn for us overnight. Every morning we American kids would go and knock on the very fragile wooden gate in front of their house. They spoke no English and we spoke no Serbo-Croatian. But they knew what we wanted and they unlocked the barn for us. But that day they were very agitated. Two of them were weeping. We didn't know what to do. And then Magda came. Magda, my God, the hottest Serbian grad student ever. I had such a thing for her, in her archeologist khaki shorts, ow...Anyway, she starts to talk to the women. It gets intense. Finally the crones go away. "What was all that?" we asked. "Well, you see, they heard we had found some bones," said Magda. "And they came out to see. They thought maybe it was someone from their family." "But this is Roman," we said. "Yes, we know that. But they..." Something passed over that beautiful face. "You see, this is in the same area where the Germans were, during the war. It is where they killed their hostages. Hundreds of them. And now they see these bones and they are saying 'It is my father. It is my husband. It is my son.' I...I think I made them understand. But if this happens again, please, be kind to them, and call me right away."

(He takes the whiskey bottle from the tackle box and knocks back a swig.)

ANGLER

You think you're so clever, dodging war, but it finds you anyway... So, we went back to the dorm and took our showers and had our dinners. And afterward I worked with Magda trying to piece together that goblet. I had hoped for an opportunity like this for weeks, to somehow get to know her, but it just wasn't in the wind that night. The next morning the VW bus dropped us off at the site and the bones were gone. Someone had come in the middle of the night and taken them all, down to the smallest ear bone. So, after all, Magda had failed to make them understand. Or maybe she had and they had just decided to mis-understand. Misunderstanding, it turns out, can be very useful. After all, did we really understand what we were doing the day before, in the trench on our hands and knees? "Scraping earth from bone," we said, but what was that earth, really? It once was flesh. Is it still? Through misunderstanding we can be...sanguine about our science. With faith in misunderstanding, at least one of the women will wear her wedding dress to the grave...That morning we

knocked again on the eggshell gate. They
came and unlocked our tools. Both sides
understood what had happened but no one
said anything. We gestured 'Thank you.'
They gestured 'You are welcome.' In the
end, we can only gesture...You know what?
Let's go see dad.

> (The Angler starts the out-
> board and puts the motor
> in gear. Wind in his hair,
> his eyes on the GPS. A very
> short run. Motor off. GPS
> beeps. Angler moves to the
> bow, removes his hat.)

ANGLER

(with great feeling)

*Full fathom five my father lies. Of his bones
are coral made. Those are pearls that were
his eyes. Nothing of him that doth fade
But doth suffer a sea-change Into something
rich and strange. Sea-nymphs hourly ring
his knell: Ding-dong. Hark! Now I hear
them, Ding-dong bell...*

> (Takes a swig of whiskey,
> then pours an offering into
> the sea.)

ANGLER

Good man. Different man. Different from
me, I mean. His generation fought Hit-

ler—my generation fought Nixon, his favorite President. Big Band—Woodstock. Frank Sinatra—Bob Dylan. I guess maybe he won that one. You don't hear Bob Dylan much anymore, at least not at shopping malls. "A hard rain's a'gonna fall..." doesn't exactly put people in a retail mood... You know, you meet guys who hate their fathers. We've all met them. Haven't spoken for years. Didn't speak, until the mad transcon dash to get bedside at the end. How sad is that? I understand the reasons, sure, what this one said, what that one did. But, God, there was literally nothing this man could have done that would make me hate him. He was my dad. You maybe don't entirely get it until you have kids of your own. I don't think any of us really consciously remember how much we depended on them, on those scared, imperfect people who raised us. "Raised us up" as they say down south. But I think you get some sense when you catch your own 2-year-old watching you. Waiting for you. Waiting for a kind word, waiting for a scolding, desperate for both. "He did it for me, now I'll do it for them." It's kind of the central equation of human nature...I was lucky. I got to be with my dad in his last hours. Both my brothers were there, too. Dad was really weak, he hadn't eaten anything for a long time, the cancer in his stomach. But when we were all gathered around, he turns to the old guy in the other bed, his suitemate, and he said: "These are my boys." I think he maybe said it just to be polite, to introduce his family. But I also heard it another way. "These are my boys." "This is what I did." "This is the product of my life." I don't know. This is the problem with being a writer—you never know how much you really hear and how much you just make up. But in this instance, I don't see that there's much difference. Dad had the chance to say one last little thing. It was a good moment either way.

LAND STATION

Securite. Securite. Securite. Coast Guard Station Long Beach has monitored a possible distress call off the Southern California Coast, Point Dume to the San Clemente Island. Two low-power transmissions occurred at 0858 and 0900. Vessels in the area are requested to keep lookout and render assistance. Coast Guard clear.

ANGLER

When you think of the arc, the changes a family goes through in its generations. Wow. I remember one year I gave my wife a birthday present. Her mother was a lovely lady, older, French Canadian, a single parent. She had had her baby late in life, as an unmarried woman, and she was never really sure who the father was. My wife knew there were three possible candidates.

So one year I bought one of those DNA kits. Where you take a cell sample from your cheek and mail it in and a month later you get the results. "You have this percentage likelihood that your parent was Northern European, Southern European, Slavic, Icelandic." And so on. Well, it was interesting, and I won't say what the results were. But in the genome report there was a fractional finding: my very white wife was possibly 1.5% sub-Saharan African. Black African. Now this didn't really mean anything. Scientifically it was insignificant, an artifact of testing or perhaps a distant echo of that sub-Saharan African who is ancestor to us all. But my kids, they thought this was fucking great! The idea, however far-fetched, that their grandfather could have been black sent them off into a frenzy of delight. For a week they were bouncing around the house, rapping, fist-bumping, "Yo, my nigger!". And I remember then, thinking back, to the Fourth of July one year, when I was in my twenties. I was visiting my dad in the small Midwestern city where he grew up. We were in the city park, at the old bandstand, and the band was pumping out "Stars and Stripes Forever" and there was beer and hot dogs and cheerleaders and old guys in old uniforms and fireworks to come. And I was feeling just very much at home. And I turned to my dad and said, "You know, this is great. The old park and the old bandstand and all." And he looks over at me, with that look of his, knowing he's going to shock me, and he says: "Yeah, the old bandstand. This is where the Klan used to meet." And then, again, with the look: "You know, we're not too many generations out of sheets."

> (Gestures—on one hand, on
> the other...)

ANGLER

Think about it. Sheets on the bandstand. "Yo, my nigger." How is it possible that this is the same family? But it is. And I don't need a $250 genetic test to prove to me that my kids are my kids. I saw them born, both of them, still the two most amazing events in my life. When my daughter appeared, I swear to God I saw my mother's face on hers. So the next time, when my son was born, I got in real close, expecting to maybe see dad's face. And my son...pissed in my face. His first act on this earth. And not his last, either. I mean, this family thing, it has its ups and downs. Your kids can make you crazy. They can break your heart. They can piss you off, they can scare you to death. And they are fucking expensive, too. But... well, like the man said: "You gonna bitch or fish?" I chose to fish.

> (The cries of seagulls and
> other marine birds. The

Angler puts his binoculars
to his eyes.)

                              ANGLER

Humm. Birds on the surface. Could be sitting on fish.

        (He fires up the outboard
        and motors off, but at low
        power.)

                              ANGLER

Try and sneak up on them.

        (A few beats later, a loud
        THUD against the hull. He
        looks overboard and sees
        something. It startles
        him.)

                              ANGLER

What the...Oh, shit....

        (He throws the skiff into
        a tight turn, powers back,
        reverses thrust. He takes
        the boathook from its hold-
        er. He leans out and uses
        the hook to latch onto
        something. He muscles it
        aboard as far as he can—
        it is a man's body, fully
        clothed, limp.)

ANGLER

Oh, no. Oh, damn....

> (He checks for a pulse, at
> the wrist, at the neck.
> He shakes his head. Then a
> wave of uncertainty, a mini
> panic attack.)

ANGLER

What do I do? I'm the guy who always knows
what to do. Okay—line.

> (He uncoils the line and,
> using the same technique he
> demonstrated on "George"
> before, he works the body
> into the skiff.)

ANGLER

Oh man, you're all burned on one side.

> (He activates the radio
> mic.)

ANGLER

Securite, securite, securite. Coast Guard
Station Long Beach, this is the fishing
skiff Uncle Jack. I have...I found...a man's
body, floating. Maybe from that Mayday. My
position is 33 degrees, 23 minutes, 65

seconds North, 118 degrees, 00 minutes, 81 seconds West. I need assistance. Over.

LAND STATION

Uncle Jack, Coast Guard Long Beach. Say again, you found a body? Over.

ANGLER

Yes, dead. He's burned. What do I do now?

CUTTER

Uncle Jack, this is the cutter Ticonderoga. We are in your vicinity. Have you secured the body? Is there any identification? Over.

ANGLER

Wait one.

> (The angler gingerly pats
> the empty pockets of the
> dead man. He glances at the
> man's groin.)

ANGLER

Ticonderoga, Uncle Jack. Negative, no ID. His fly is up.

CUTTER

Say again?

>ANGLER

I said...Never mind. Over.

>CUTTER

Stand by on 16.

>ANGLER

Uncle Jack, standing by.

>(The angler sits and looks
>at his new passenger for
>several beats.)

>ANGLER

Well, you finally found me, didn't you? All those times I lied about you and now here you are. I never wanted to be a pussy, see. Everybody else...All the stories I heard from friends, from George and the other guys who went to 'Nam, from cops I know. I never wanted to be a pussy, so I made up stories, dead people I had seen and touched: the car accident in college, the dead homeless guy on the street. But it was all bullshit. I never did, see one. A dead one. A dead Homo Sapiens. I don't mean all tarted up in a coffin. I mean dead, in the street, in the mud, soaked in sea water. I never did, 'til now. I think I...I've kind of been waiting for you...There was Jay but I just missed Jay. My friend Jay, he died in his sleep. The paramedics were just pulling away with his body when I got there. The landlord knew I was a friend so she let me into his apartment. To look for numbers of next of kin, and so on, but I never saw his body. Jay was the guy...we all know the guy...came to Hollywood to be in 'the industry' and never even got close enough to be teased by it. He never won the bet—not first, not biggest, not most. He did find a honking big gold nugget once, though...I found Jay's Ipod that morning. I turned it on and brought up the last song he had been listening to. The night before. Maybe as he went to sleep. It was the Rolling Stones' "You Can't Always Get What You Want." You know it, right? "You can't always get what you want, But if you try sometimes, You just might find, You get what you need."

CUTTER

Uncle Jack, we have you visual.

(Angler moves close to the body. In a whisper...)

ANGLER

So, my friend...Did you get what you need-ed? Did you have the chance, to say one

last little thing? Tell me now—I'm listening.

> (Leans closer still. The
> sound of a large vessel ap-
> proaching.)

ANGLER

Okay....

> (Sound of the cutter along-
> side.)

CUTTER

Uncle Jack, we're coming abeam your port
side.

ANGLER

Understood, Ticonderoga. How do you want
to do this?

CUTTER

Make a line fast to him and heave it over.

> (Angler checks that his
> line is securely tied to
> the body and heaves the
> bitter end over.)

CUTTER

We will need for you to follow us into the station, so we can take your statement.

                              ANGLER

Okay, he's secure. Haul away.

          (The line tightens and the
          body is dragged away.)

                              CUTTER

Did you understand, Uncle Jack, you need to follow us in? Over.

                              ANGLER

Affirmative. I'll get underway in just a minute.

                              CUTTER

Very well. Ticonderoga moving off. Clear.

          (The sound of the cutter
          departing. The angler takes
          a deep breath, then starts
          preparing the skiff for the
          run into harbor. He secures
          the boathook and rods. He
          closes his tackle box. He
          puts on his life preserver.
          He looks around, checking.
          Decides there is one last
          task. He digs into the fish

locker and comes up with
the limp Never Die.)

                    ANGLER

You didn't die on me, did you?

        (He kneels over the tran-
        som where he set the red
        snapper free and starts the
        same procedure.)

                    ANGLER

Come on...Let's get those gills working...
Come on...Come on....

        (But it is not working.
        Abruptly the day's com-
        pounding emotions over-
        come him. Sudden tears fill
        his eyes, profound regret
        cracks his voice.)

                    ANGLER

Come on...Please....

        (The unseen fish responds.)

                    ANGLER

All right! That's it. And...gone!

        ("You Can't Always Get What
        You Want" [Jagger vocal cue]

starts to play softly. The
angler dries his eyes. He
looks into the water, profoundly grateful. He crosses
to the VHF.)

ANGLER

Ticonderoga, this is Uncle Jack. Under
way now. I will follow you in. Uncle Jack
clear.

(He looks into the sea one
more time.)

ANGLER

Chucklehead....

(He starts the outboard and
throttles up as lights fade
and music swells.)

END